Martin Kirk Griggs

Lyrics of the Lariat

Poems with Notes

Martin Kirk Griggs

Lyrics of the Lariat
Poems with Notes

ISBN/EAN: 9783744788328

Printed in Europe, USA, Canada, Australia, Japan

Cover: Foto ©Andreas Hilbeck / pixelio.de

More available books at **www.hansebooks.com**

LYRICS OF THE LARIAT

POEMS WITH NOTES

BY

NATHAN KIRK GRIGGS

FLEMING H. REVELL COMPANY
NEW YORK—CHICAGO—TORONTO

The Lakeside Press
R. R. DONNELLEY & SONS CO., CHICAGO

PREFACE.

Plain prose is Jersey cream,
   From stony vessel dipt,
While poetry is froth,
   By silver ladle whipt;

And tho' the one will give
   Great stores of bread and meat,
The other rarely yields
   A blessed thing to eat.

CONTENTS.

CONTENTS.

The Cowboy.'

With eyes that were blazing,
But now that are glazing,
In barroom, "The Bruin"—that rattlesnake den—
A cowboy is lying,
And silent, is dying,
Surrounded by careless, yet resolute men.

So, sing of the rover,
Whose wand'rings are over,
And who, without even a tremor of dread,
Lies down on the prairie,
Where nature makes merry,
And spears of the cactus are guarding his bed.

HO' father and mother,
And even one other,
Had begged him to tarry, they pleaded in vain;
For wild as a ranger,
And mocking at danger,
He cared but to gallop, a Knight of the Plain.

Tho' zephyrs were creeping,
Or tempests were leaping,
The spur, to the bronco, he wantonly prest;
And shouting and singing,
And lariat swinging,
Rode on like a spirit that never knew rest.

Wherever he wandered,
His money he squandered,
With hand of a gambler and kingliest grace;
And ever was willing
To stake his last shilling
On turn of a penny or chance of an ace.

A hand to the weary,
And smile to the dreary,
He willingly offered to lowliest woe;
And taunt to the sneering,
And blow to the jeering,
As willingly tendered to insolent **foe.**

Last night, at The Bruin,
He guzzled red ruin,
And tackled draw poker, along with the rest;
When one began stealing
The cards they were dealing,
And waddy objecting, was shot in the breast.

Aware that he's going,
For cold he is growing,
He calls for his saddle as rest for his head;
Then says, without flinching,
That "Death is now sinching,"
And then, on his blanket, the puncher lies dead.

So, sing in soft numbers,
Of him that now slumbers,
Who wantoned with fortune and scouted at care;
And sweetly is dreaming,
Tho' curlews are screaming,
And coyotēs howling like imps of despair.

Vesper Cradle Song.

Now the day at prayer is kneeling,
  Hushabye, baby, sleep;
And the vesper notes are stealing,
  Hushabye, baby, sleep;
And the eve, in silver, drest,
Pins her star upon her breast;
    Sing low, swing low,
    Hushabye, baby, sleep.

Now the day is drowsy growing,
  Hushabye, baby, sleep;
And the firefly lamps are glowing,
  Hushabye, baby, sleep;
And the lily sips, for you,
Nectar from the lips of dew;
    Sing low, swing low,
    Hushabye, baby, sleep.

Now the day is sweetly dreaming,
  Hushabye, baby, sleep;
And the eyes of night are beaming,
  Hushabye, baby, sleep;
And beside your cherub feet,
Pussy purrs to you, my sweet;
  Sing low, swing low,
  Hushabye, baby, sleep.

The Waters to the Hosts.

As laughing brooklet goes
   To join the noble stream,
Or dallies with the birds,
   That e'er its lovers seem,
Or tarries, here and there,
   To kiss the bending flow'rs,
It ever sweetly sings,
   In happy, holy hours:
     Ye Hosts above,
      The Lord is Love.

As smiling river greets
  The pure and lowly stream,
Or ripples, while the stars
  Above in beauty beam,
Or journeys swiftly on
  To reach the rolling main,
It ever sweetly sings,
  That rhythmic, rich refrain:
    Ye Hosts above,
      The Lord is Love.

As boundless ocean hails
  The broad and mighty stream,
Or glistens, while the sails
  Upon its bosom gleam,
Or surges, while the wind
  In solemn cadence moans,
It ever sweetly sings,
  In tender, touching tones:
    Ye Hosts above,
      The Lord is Love.

And long as brooklet runs
  To wed the courtly stream,
And long as river seeks
  The coral caves to dream,
And long as ocean swells,
  With pulse and purpose strong,
They yet will sweetly sing
  That same seraphic song:
    Ye Hosts above,
      The Lord is Love.

Love's many strange moods
  Are blossoms of passion,
That Will cannot grow,
  Nor Reason may fashion;
But Fancy alone,
  Gives birth to the flowers,
That burst into life,
  In Cupid's wild bowers.

Ben.[2]

S many boys have
longed to do,
And many boys have
done,
When in my teens, I drifted West,
To find where wealth
was won;
And anchored soon where
men were tough,
As tough as earth could
boast,
Where each it seemed, had
volunteered
To serve in Satan's host.

Among the number there was one
  They called the "Devil's Ace,"
A fellow with a sorrel top,
  And yellow, freckled face;
Whose wrath was like the fiery floods
  That sweep the rolling plain,
With fury that no tongue may tell,
  Nor mortal arm restrain.

Another one was "Saintly Sam,"
  A coy, but gamey bird,
Who rarely steamed above his gauge,
  And rarer cussed a word;
And yet whose heart was like the wild,
  Where spears of cactus grow,
And he that dared to trespass there,
  Received a stinging blow.

And one was dubbed as " Whiskey Jack,"
  A brutal, brawling bloat,
Who'd meanly thump the tenderfoot,
  Then o'er his anguish gloat;
And there were Buck and Booze and Blood,
  Who had no thought of fame,
And yet, in way of wickedness,
  Deserved an honored name.

But there was one among the crowd,
  I only knew as " Ben;"
Who stood a notch above the rest
  Of all those rowdy men;
Who was a brawny, burly chap,
  The master soul of sin,
And where the others called a halt,
  He'd just about begin.

In every spree he'd be the one
  To down the most of budge;
And as to who had won at cards,
  He'd always be the judge;
In short, he was a Hercules,
  A sort of pagan boss,
Who made the other heathen bow,
  And worship him as Joss.

For such a harum - scarum lot,
  Of course my gait was slow;
And then, I thought the track they took
  Was pointed straight below;
Besides, I'd vowed, when yet a kid,
  And pledged my mother, too,
That I would never taste the truck
  She said the demons brew.

It chanced the day I landed there,
  That some one set them up;
When I, with fears and yet with thanks,
  Declined the proffered cup;
And then I thought my time had come,
  Because the others said,
That if I didn't hoist it in,
  They'd load my hulk with lead.

At this, big Ben — God save his soul!
  Stretched forth his arm of law,
And told each guzzler in the gang,
  To cease to wag the jaw;
And then he turned to me and asked,
  In way that sounded queer,
The why it was I then refused
  To take a drop of cheer.

Tho' fairly quaking in my boots,
    I yet had nerve enough,
To tell them why I'd vowed the vow
    To never taste the stuff;
And how, till then, I'd kept my word,
    In spite of jeer and scoff,
And therefore hoped they condescend
    To kindly let me off.

Then O, it seemed so good to hear
    The precious words of Ben,
As savagely, with blazing eyes,
    He faced the scowling men,
And swore, by all the blessed saints,
    He'd plug the imp of sin,
Who dared to lay a hand on me
    To make me swig the gin.

And then, he said, in lower tones,
  A mother once he'd had,
Who tried her best, but died too soon,
  To raise a decent lad;
And then he hissed, between his teeth,
  He thought I'd acted square,
And that the whelp who disagreed,
  Would climb the golden stair.

And then the others called the turn,
  And said they wept for joy,
To find a chap — who hadn't wings—
  That yet was mother's boy;
Indeed, I guess, tho' strange it was,
  A couple even cried,
I reckon just because of her
  Who Ben declared had died.

And, odd to say, they caved around,
  With navy in each hand,
And said the one who filled me up,
  Would hunt the hotter land;
And odder too, they formed a ring,
  And raised their hands and swore,
That if I dared to break my pledge,
  They sure would hunt my gore.

As now I conjure back the scene,
  And live again the day,
That Ben stood there, and cussed and cussed,
  And kept those wolves at bay,
I swear he seems a Moses sent
  To sternly plead my cause,
And show to all those wretched men,
  The might of holy laws.

Just what the Lord should do with Ben,
  There is, of course, a doubt;
But still, I think, the righteous One,
  Should hardly bar him out;
At least, when I have reached the gate, .
  Where Peter holds the key,
You bet your life I'll plead for Ben,
  As Ben once pled for me.

A Cur.

An orator, with tongue of fire,
　Denounced the deed of one,
Who scowled the while the polished ire
　In burning satire run;
When suddenly, in voice that told
　The keenness of the slur,
The latter cried, in manner bold:
　And dare you call me 'cur?'

The speaker paused, but not with fear,
　And scanned the glaring foe,
Then made reply, with cynic sneer,
　In measured tones and slow:
By all the joys, when sorrows end,
　No dog I called you, sir,
Because no whelp will wound a friend,
　And you're unlike the cur.

The dog that jogs before your wheels,
　　When riches holds the reins,
Will trot behind your heavy heels,
　　Nor heed your pauper chains;
Nor yet will he your hovel fly,
　　Tho' hunger drives the spur,
And so 'tis plain the reason why
　　I shrink to call you 'cur.'

And so your dog, of golden days,
　　When all your worth proclaim,
Will share your lot, tho' songs of praise,
　　Give place to dirge of blame;
And should you sleep in dungeon dread,
　　No shame would him deter,
But there he'd go to guard your bed;—
　　Who'd think to call you 'cur?'

My prattling maid, a witching fay,
  My angel four-year-old,
Went forth to play, one summer day,
  And tripped where waters rolled;
When quickly sprang her shaggy mate.
  And lost his life for her;
And both for me, in Heaven wait;—
  D'you think I'd call you 'cur?'

More swift than the light,
Sun-winged on its flight,
More swift than the flash,
When thunder-clouds clash,
Mind flies to life's morn,
  And brings to the old,
  When youth they behold,
Dead scenes, newly born.

The flowers of love spring up in our highways,
And wave in our fields and border our byways,
And yet we ne'er learn who plants them nor tills
    them,
Nor yet, when they die, what secret foe kills them.

Some flowers of love, tho' carefully tended,
And from the rude blast, by fond ones defended,
Bloom sweetly an hour, then wither and perish,
And leave not a leaf for fond ones to cherish.

And other love-blooms are beautiful roses,
That blossom from spring, till summer-time closes;
And then only fade, because we neglect them,
And from the chill frost, we fail to protect them.

And other love-blooms, tho' fragile and lowly,
Are jewels of earth, most precious and holy;
For even when winds, of Autumn, are sighing,
Those flowers bloom on, unfading, undying.

Those blooms of the heart, that gladden life's
    mountains,
Are watered by rills that flow from pure fountains;
And tho' a white shroud, in winter, conceals them,
An angel again, in spring-time, reveals them.

haste to the Mount of the Lord.

Tho' the dark flags of the tempest are streaming.
  Waved by the hosts of the sky,
And the bright blades o'er the ramparts are gleaming,
  Flashed by the cohorts on high, —
Tho' the gray steeds of the winter are leaping,
  Crazed by the lash of the air,
And the wan earth in its surplice is sleeping,
  Hushed by the dirge of Despair,
Still, on the height, and removed from all sorrow,
  Stung by no chastening rod,
Safe may we be, on the beautiful morrow,
  Bathed in the sunlight of God;
So, to the One, who is lovingly calling,
  Sing we a song in accord,
And, when the shadows of danger are falling,
  Haste to the Mount of the Lord.

Tho' the rare buds that in childhood we cherished,
    Died in the morning of June,
And the ripe fruits of affection have perished,
    Seared by the glare of the noon,—
Tho' the dear friends all around us are paling,
    Chilled by the breath of the frost,
And the low notes of remembrance are wailing,
    Winged o'er the breasts of our lost,
Still, on the height, and beset by no sorrow,
    Scourged by no chastening rod,
Glad may we be, on the beautiful morrow,
    Kissed by the sunlight of God;
So, to the One, who is tenderly calling,
    Breathe we a prayer in accord,
And, when the waters of anguish are falling,
    Haste to the Mount of the Lord.

Maverick Joe.[a]

DON'T know
    Of Maverick Joe,
That buster of broncos in chief,
      And who,
    As every one knew,
Waxed rich as a Maverick thief?

    It's strange,
    Out here on the range,
That you haven't known of his name,
      Nor heard
    How ranchers were stirred
Because of his Maverick fame.

BRONCO-BUSTER.

Well, then,
I'll whisper again,
That tale of the cow and her kid,
Altho',
Thought Maverick Joe,
The trick was a corker they did.

Out West,
With lucre unblest,
He rangled for others a year,
While budge,
As well you may judge,
Occasion'ly offered him cheer.

One day,
With poker the play—
That game by no tenderfoot learned—
I hear
He rustled a steer,
That wasn't quite honestly earned.

And then,

He built him a den,

Way out where the punchers were few,

And there,

Tho' not by the square,

He soon to a cattle-king grew.

'Twas queer

How often that steer

Raised calves for his Maverick "+" (cross),

Tho' now,

I'm bound to allow,

His gain was some other one's loss.

One noon,

Along about June,

A Maverick daisy he saw—

The best,

And one that he guessed

He'd own by the Maverick law.

And so
He rastled it low,
And gave it a touch of his brand,
Then smiled,
For fortune beguiled,
That happiest chump in the land.

Next morn,
As sure as I'm born,
It chanced that a round-up begun,
And then,
Some blundering men,
Caught on to the caper he'd done.

For now,
They circled a cow,
One bearing a "□" (square) on her side,
That bawled,
And motherly called,
At sight of his Maverick pride.

The kid
Then bellowed and slid,
And buckled right in for a meal;
And — well,
It's idle to tell
The feelings he couldn't conceal.

Tho' caught,
He swore it was bought,
Where never a seller was nigh;
But all,
Tho' praising his gall,
Yet reckoned no cattle would lie.

And thus,

That ornery cuss

Got sinched on account of that pair;

Because,

By cattlemen laws,

A "✛" shouldn't tackle a "▢".

SABBATH MORN.

Like scenes of youth, to the wand'ring one,
Like hours of rest, when the task is done,
Like dreams of health, when the lips grow pale,
Like hearth of home, when the drear winds wail,
   Is Sabbath Morn.

Like white of sail, on the lonely deep,
Like wand of hope, when the troubles sweep,
Like gleam of gold, when the clouds are rent,
Like hush of peace, when the storm is spent,
   Is Sabbath Morn.

Like kiss of sleep, when the day is o'er,
Like face of friend, on an alien shore,
Like draught of dew, to the fainting bloom,
Like balm of faith, at the closing tomb,
   Is Sabbath Morn.

Like notes of joy, in a dirge of sighs,
Like songs of old, when the daylight dies,
Like glimpse of stream, in a waste of sand,
Like touch of love, from a dear one's hand,
         Is Sabbath Morn.

Rays of beauty floated round me,
  And my world seemed fairyland,
When the shutters of my fancy,
  Wide were swung by Cupid's hand;
Then the chalice of my gladness,
  Glowed and sparkled in my sun,
While I drained its holy nectar,
  Quaffed to him, my plighted one;—
Marvel not my day of dreaming,
  Marvel not nor query when,
For I can but give you answer:
  It was then, then, then.

When the noonday light is guarding,
  Who may say when dawn begun?
And when midnight gloom is warding,
  Who may say when eve was done?

So, when Love has winged his arrow,
    Who may say when bow he bent?
And when Love afar has journeyed,
    Who may say the time he went?—
Marvel not my day of dreaming,
    Marvel not nor query when,
For I can but give you answer:
    It was then, then, then.

When I heard that olden story,
    Told by Love with master skill,
Like a siren song it wooed me,
    Thralled me with a siren will;
And tho' far away I've wandered,
    From that day of perfect bliss,
Still, a wand of sweet enchantment,
    Blends, somehow, that time with this;—
Marvel not my day of dreaming,
    Marvel not nor query when,

For I can but give you answer:
  It was then, then, then.

As the rarest chords of pleasure,
  Die at times, in minor strains,
And the silv'ry haze of summer,
  Fades away in autumn rains,
So, the one, my soul exalted,
  Of whose life I seemed a part,
Wafted me to heights of rapture,
  Then threw down my trusting heart;—
Marvel not my day of dreaming,
  Marvel not nor query when,
For I can but give you answer:
  It was then, then, then.

The Prairie-Dog.[5]

I'm a merry prairie-dog,
    Yip, yip, yip,
And, like a jolly pollywog,
    Flip, flip, flip;
And when I give my little yip,
Why then I flip my little tail,
And when I give my tail a flip,
Why then to yip I never fail;
And thus I ever gayly bark,
    Yip, yip, yip,
And ever on my daily lark,
    Flip, flip, flip.

And I reside in squatter-town,
Where even corner lots are free,
And I'm no common country clown,
Altho' somewhat of low degree;
For I'm a merry prairie-dog,
  Yip, yip, yip,
And, like a jolly pollywog,
  Flip, flip, flip.

And I'm a great aristocrat,
And will admit that I am vain,
But never wear a dudey hat,
Nor sport a razzle-dazzle cane;
For I'm a merry prairie-dog,
  Yip, yip, yip,
And, like a jolly pollywog,
  Flip, flip, flip.

And though I rule the city roost,
And have the aldermanic skill,
I never give my lot a boost,
And make another foot the bill:
And thus I ever gayly bark,
　　　Yip, yip, yip,
And ever, on my daily lark,
　　　Flip, flip, flip.

And tho' the snakes I often see,
I never go on any toots,
And not a soul can say of me,
That I have snakes within my boots;
And thus I ever gayly bark,
　　　Yip, yip, yip,
And ever on my daily lark,
　　　Flip, flip, flip.

And I've a judge with owly eyes,
Who helps the serpent lawyers thro',
And sits around, appearing wise,
As little judges always do;
And thus I ever gayly bark,
    Yip, yip, yip,
And ever on my daily lark,
    Flip, flip, flip.

And I'm a chap, I surely think,
About as cute as other men,
For when I want to get a drink,
I simply scoot within my den;
And thus I ever gayly bark,
    Yip, yip, yip,
And ever, on my daily lark,
    Flip, flip, flip.

O, I'm a merry prairie-dog,
    Yip, yip, yip,
And, like a jolly pollywog,
    Flip, flip, flip;
And I'm the dandy of the west,
And yip and yip my mellow rhyme,
And as my tail declines to rest,
I flip and flip in even time;
And thus I ever gayly bark,
    Yip, yip, yip,
And ever, on my daily lark,
    Flip, flip, flip.

Our Flag.

Of all the numberless flags
    unfurled,
Thro'out this hurrying,
    restless world,
The beautiful one we love
    to view,
That banner of stars, on field of blue,
Is far to the front upon the sea
Of boundless and deep prosperity.

LITTLE FOXES

Keep back the angry frowns, dear maid,
    For none but laughing eyes,
        And smiling lips, and heart so gay,
        And childish glee, from day to day,
    Are what your parents prize;
Keep back the angry frowns, dear maid,
For angry frowns make beauty fade.

Keep back the hasty words, my dear,
    For well you surely know,
        That even tho' you strive for aye,
        You never can those words unsay,
    If once they rudely go;
Keep back the hasty words, my dear,
For hasty words will cause a tear.

Drive out your evil thoughts, dear boy,
  For none will ever bring,
    To wounded heart, the balm of prayer,
    Nor ever drive away a care,
  Nor make hosannas ring;
Drive out your evil thoughts, dear boy,
For evil thoughts ne'er lead to joy.

Drive out your little sins, my child,
  For like the nearing night,
    They surely yet will darker grow,
    And ever gloom your way with woe,
  And all your future blight;
Drive out your little sins, my child,
For little sins are all defiled.

THE GENII OF WINE

The Genii of Wine.

O the rosy wine is blushing,
   Like a ruby, kissed with light;
O the ringing, thrilling music,
   Makes the dreary hours grow bright;
O the dizzy, dreamy dancing,
   True and loving hearts enthrall;
O the artful, luring sirens,
   Seem the angels of the ball;
Ah! the sirens and the dancing,
   And the music and the wine,
Are the spirits of the revel,
   That the foolish deem divine;
But the wanton smiles of pleasure,
   Soon will vanish, chased by sneers,
And the fragile cup of gladness,
   Soon be running o'er with tears.

O the blushing wine is glowing,
　　Like the ruddy cheeks of mirth;
O the lovely, costly mirrors
　　Seem reflecting only worth;
O the pleasing, princely paintings
　　Seem enchanting as a smile;
O the winning, wooing billiards
　　Seem repeating, " Pause awhile;"—
Ah! the billiards and the paintings,
　　And the mirrors and the wine,
Are so charming that the careless,
　　To their magic oft resign;
But that stately hall of splendor,
　　So beguiling, so sublime,
Is a reeking hot-house only,
　　Filled with springing shoots of crime.

O the glowing wine is glaring,
 Like the dragon eyes of hate;
O the reckless, frenzied gambler
 Is defying God and fate;
O the brainless, brutal brawler
 Is inviting pain and shame;
O the worthless, sotted beggar
 Is profaning manhood's name;—
Ah! the begger and the brawler
 And the gambler and the wine,
Are companions worthy, only,
 Those attending Pluto's shrine;
But the drunkard, witched to madness,
 By a strangely potent spell,
Gropes forever in their darkness,
 Sinks forever in their hell.

O the glaring wine is burning,
　　Like the wasting fires of woe;
O the deadly, gleaming dagger
　　Gives the wanton, wicked blow;
O the dismal, darksome dungeon,
　　Is awakened by no prayer;
O the awful, fearful scaffold
　　Tells of hopeless, black despair;—
Ah! the scaffold and the dungeon,
　　And the dagger and the wine,
Are the ripened fruits of satan—
　　Aye, thou demon, they are thine!—
But, poor drunkard, child of weakness,
　　Yours the anguish not alone,
For your kinsmen, too, must harvest
　　From the sorrows you have grown.

SHIPS of STATE

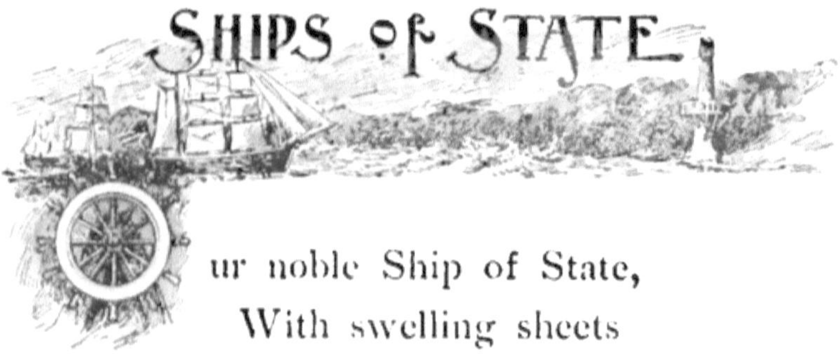

Our noble Ship of State,
    With swelling sheets
    The soft wind greets,
    And spreads her sails,
    Despite the gales,
And swiftly bears the Free;
While others' ships, tho' great.
    If zephyrs go,
    Or breezes blow,
    With canvas wide
    Yet slowly glide,
Upon the golden Sea.

There is a Sun, so bright, so bright,
That floods my sky with morning light,
And ever lends me rays, soft rays,
To cheer me on my rugged ways,
And ever I am drawn above,
By that dear Sun, my Dream of Love.

There is a World, divine, divine,
Where trust has reared a golden shrine,
And all is filled with joy, pure joy,
And cares come not, nor pleasures cloy,
And ever I am drawn above,
By that dear World, my Dream of Love.

There is a Star, so clear, so clear,
That smiles upon my pathway drear,
And gives to life a wing, swift wing,
With which to soar where angels sing,
And ever I am drawn above,
By that dear Star, my Dream of Love.

There is a Moon, serene, serene,
That robes the earth with silver sheen,
And thrills the dales of gloom, deep gloom,
And paints a tint on ev'ry bloom,
And ever I am drawn above,
By that dear Moon, my Dream of Love.

There is a Heart, more true, more true,
Than yet was sung, or seraph knew,—
My Sun and World, my Light, sweet Light,
My Star and Moon, my lone Delight,—
And ever I am drawn above,
By that dear Heart, **my Dream of Love.**

So Sam, old boy, you were East the day
That awful storm came across this way,
With swinging tread, and a blast of woe,
From up there North, where the Blizzards grow;
But still you read quite enough, I guess,
About that spell, in the down-east press,
For motes out here, make the chaps there, cry,
While beams, down there, never make them sigh;
And let the feet of a cyclone swing,
And trip our turf with a highland fling,
Or let us wink to the chap, Judge Lynch,
To treat some whelp to a neck-tie sinch,
And down it goes, in their blackguard type,

And thus the West gets a back-hand swipe;—
　　And, Sam, no doubt for the dauntless
　　　Nell,
　　　You threw your hat, with a
　　　　cowboy yell,
　　　On reading how, in the
　　　　blinding snow,
　　　She kept the boys
　　　and the girls
　　　in tow,

And brought
　them home,
　　tho' the storm-
　　winds dread,
Like devils, clutched
　at the school she led.
And then, I'll wage that
　you raised one shout,

For her that taught where the wood gave out,
Whose flock she kept in the room all night,
Tho' air grew chill and there gleamed no light,
And with them romped, nor allowed them sleep,
For fear Death's arms would around them creep.
But for that girl, on the cold North Loup,
The one that taught in the old sod-coop,
Who saved the kids, ev'ry blessed one,
Then died herself when the job was done,
I'll bet my boots that your sobbing heart,
Somehow, old chap, made the tear-drops start.

But, Sam, one thing, I presume, at least,
You did not read when away down East,
For no one there, ever wrote or knew
How Hank got home, when the mad winds blew,
And so I'll tell of the tramp he had,
Steered on alone, by his own brave lad.
Before that storm, tho' the world seemed glad,
The sunlight shone in a way half sad,

For straggling flakes, with a careless flight,
Came floating down, in the soft, weird light,
And sailed about, in the warm, sweet air,
With sun-gold twined in their snow-white hair,
Then gently fell, with a languid grace,
And veiled the face of the earth with lace,
And not a twig by a breeze was stirred,
And, Sam, no threat of a storm was heard.

At three that day, or about that time,
While love yet crooned o'er the slumb'ring clime,
There came a sound, o'er the sun-lit plain,
Like distant roar of a railway train,
And then the hosts, from the Blizzard's lair,
Sprang forth, full-armed, on their steeds of air,
And, urged by Death, came a thund'ring down,
With scowls as black as a demon's frown,
And bowling on, like a thousand steers,
Whose eyes are bulged, and ablaze with fears.

And then, concealed by the clouds they spread,
At once they charged, with an earthquake tread,
And shrieking, leaped at the drowsing sky,
And bore it down with a fiendish cry;
And cursing, smote with an iron hand,
The blanching cheek of the quaking land;
And frothing, stamped on the prey they slew,
Then wailed a dirge as they onward flew.

Well, Sam, that noon, as he always did,
Hank romped awhile with the tow-head kid—
That six-year-old, little pug-nosed tod,
Who ruled his ranch with a wizard's rod—
Then gave the lad a resounding smack,
And told his wife he would soon be back,
And whistling loud, to the fields was gone,
Without his gloves, nor a thick coat on,
And thus he was when the drunken snow
Came reeling in with the hosts of woe.

Now, when Hank's wife saw the storm rush in,
With brow as black as the soul of sin,
She cried with fright, like a woman would,
Then grabbed her shawl, and her warm, knit hood,
And thus prepared,—'twas an insane prank,—
She sought to go on a search for Hank.

Just then the lad, like a wayward elf,
Got up and joined in the cry himself,
And held her dress, and declared he knew
His pa would come when his work was thro';
And then he smiled, in a trustful way,
And said: I'll ring, and mamma, you pray,
And then he'll hear, and he'll think he's late,
And come right home, for he'll know we wait.
Now, Sam, what else could the poor thing do,
While Furies raved and the cohorts flew,
Than kneel and pray to the one Great One,
To steer Hank home to herself and son?

So down she got and at once sailed in,
Just like one does when the stakes he'd win;
And, Sam, I guess, in her wild despair,
She held four kings at the game of prayer.

The boy, ere this, with a brave, strong heart,
Had hopped upstairs to perform his part,
And, in less time than a man dare tell,

       Had reached the cord of
        the big farm-bell,
      And pulled and pulled, till
        it creaked and swung,
      Then yanked and yanked,
        while it rung and rung;—

And, Sam, right here, I'll remark one thing,
That those great bells, in the towns, now ring,
Alone, I think, just to kill sick folks,
For not one soul to the church they coax;
Their senseless clang, when the world's at rest,
Appears to me like a wanton jest;—

But Hank's big bell never tolled but joy,
And so that day, for that precious boy,
It sent Hank cheer, thro' the grizzly gloom,
And, in his heart, made the hope-buds bloom.
Now, when the troops, spurred along by Death,
Came charging down on the Whirlwind's breath,
Hank gave one look, with a wild surprise,
Then swifter flew than the greyhound flies,
But paused, ere long, for the seething frost
So filled his eyes that his course he lost;
Now, while he stood, and the Blizzard jeered,
And gloating imps at their victim leered,
He heard the voice of the wooing bell,
Come floating on, with a wondrous swell,
As ring the tones from the heav'nly dome:
" Your loved ones wait, hurry home, come home;"—
I'll grant that Fame, with her lies and wiles,
Can lure her dupes where delight ne'er smiles,
That scowling Hate, with its madd'ning spell,
Can drive some souls to the depths of hell,

That Gold — that king of the heartless reign —
Can steel his serfs to the cries of pain,
Yet, Sam, true love has a ʻforce or will
That shames those slaves of the realms of ill;
So, when that voice, thro' the whirling foam,
Came floating down with that prayer from home,
Hank's mind flew on to the loved ones there,
Then full he turned on the ranks of air,
And fiercely on to the northward prest,
Tho' ice-shot rained on his thin-clad breast,
Nor stayed his feet in the sleet-bound grass,
Tho' legions fired in his face with glass,
Nor changed his course, nor with fear once quailed,
Tho' blind the way, and his strength then failed.

But, Sam, no tongue on the earth can tell
Just how Hank tramped to that pleading bell,
And so I'll skip from the gloom and roar,
And say he fell, thro' his own wide door,
For Death, right there, tripped his stone-like feet,

Then slunk away, with his winding-sheet;—
Then, Sam, gewhizz, but the prayer stopped then,
Without a hint of the word "Amen;"
And that big bell, that the brave boy swung,
Just creaked, "Hank's here," then it held its tongue;
And that wide door, with a slam, went to,
And shut the wrath of the storm from view.
Then, when he'd thawed, you can bet your life,
He hugged that lad and he kissed that wife;
And she, poor soul, why she cried and cried,
As tho,' in truth, that her Hank had died;
But that strange kid, tho' he wept some, too,
Just said, "Say, Pa, was your work all thro'?"

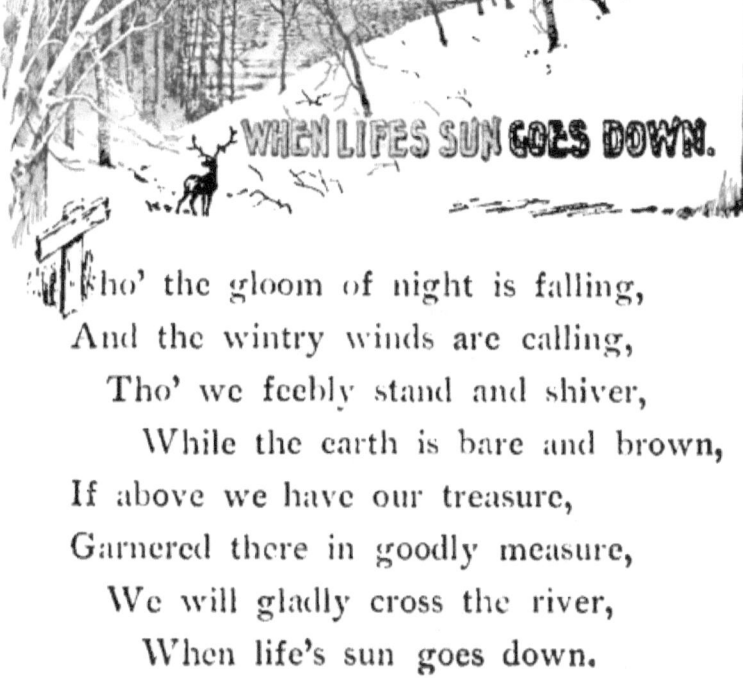

WHEN LIFES SUN GOES DOWN.

Tho' the gloom of night is falling,
And the wintry winds are calling,
  Tho' we feebly stand and shiver,
    While the earth is bare and brown,
If above we have our treasure,
Garnered there in goodly measure,
  We will gladly cross the river,
    When life's sun goes down.

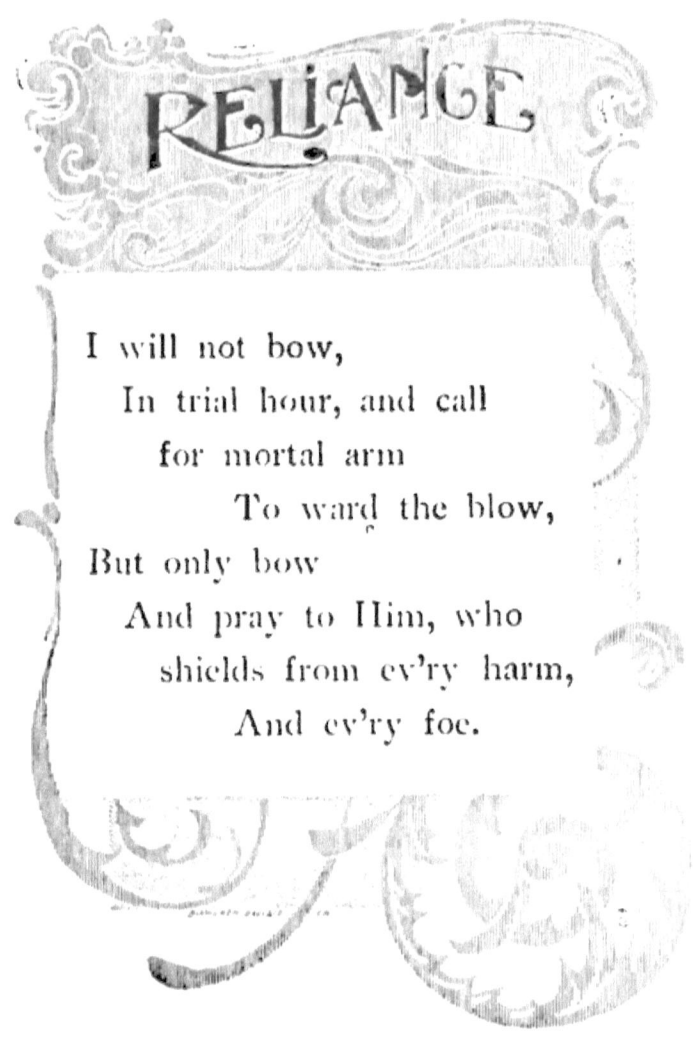

RELIANCE

I will not bow,
   In trial hour, and call
     for mortal arm
       To ward the blow,
But only bow
   And pray to Him, who
     shields from ev'ry harm,
      And ev'ry foe.

SERPENTS.

 THOUSAND boughs are bending,
  Within the woodland wild,
  As softly bends a mother
Above her slumb'ring child;
And tiny brooks are sporting,
  Where elves their vigils keep,
As children sport, at ev'ning,
  Ere hushed by wand of sleep;
And dainty blooms are blushing,
  With tints from realms of bliss,
As maidens blush with rapture,
  When lovers steal a kiss;—
Ah, surely, 'mid such beauty,
  Where Peace unfolds her wing,
A serpent is not lurking,
  To dart a deadly sting;—

Not so, for here the foe,
  With poisoned tongue of Satan,
    Lies low
      To strike the blow.

A humble home is ringing,
  With joyful notes of song,
Awaking, with their gladness,
  No dread nor thought of wrong;
And happy boys are dreaming
  Of place and honored name,
And thinking that a nation
  May yet their worth proclaim;
And smiling girls are trusting,
  That life, with them, will be
As river, gliding, gently,
  To find the silv'ry sea;—

Ah, surely, 'mid such pleasure,
    Where Love unfolds her wing,
A serpent is not lurking,
    To dart a deadly sting;—
Not so, for here the foe,
    With venomed tongue of Satan,
        Lies low
            To strike the blow.

A woman proud, is singing,
    And throngs acclaim her thrall,
And hail the magic numbers
    That chain the hearts of all;
And statesmen wise, are speaking
    The words that woo and thrill,

And forcing, with their logic,
　The world to do their will;
And warriors bold, are leading,
　Where Horror shrieks and raves,
And gaining, by the carnage,
　The wreath that hero craves;—
Ah, surely, 'mid such power,
　Where Fame unfolds her wing,
A serpent is not lurking,
　To dart a deadly sting;—
Not so, for here the foe,
　With forked tongue of Satan,
　　　Lies low
　　　To strike the blow.

THE DESERTED CHURCH

THE DESERTED CHURCH.

There's an old gray church, deserted and lone —
   Where, fondly, the ivy yet clings —
Whose glory is gone, and spirit has flown,
   And never to worship now rings;
Nor ever the strains of beautiful lay,
   Re-echo enchantingly there,
But only the wind's weird wailings to-day,
   Awaken that sanctum of prayer.
     O, hallowed Church, so dear,
Thy ivy-clad walls I'm longing again to see,
     And thy roof, by moss o'ergrown,
     And thy floor, of slabs and stone,
For memory fond now carries me back to thee.

Up aloft, in gloom, in wondering dome,
　The church-bell, corroding, is dumb,
Where swallows have found, in quiet, a home,
　And owlets, in safety, have come ;
And sweetly, for years, the sexton, so brave,
　Has rested with those he laid low,
And over his breast, the willow-boughs wave,
　And lovely forget me-nots blow.
　　O, hallowed Church, so dear,
Thy sorrowing notes, that often awoke the dell,
　　Were attuned, by hands above,
　　To inspire, by tones of love,
The mourner to sigh the answer of faith; 'Tis well.

When the star, of day, has faded from sight,
　And darkness its banner unfurled,

And pickets, on high, in armor so bright,
  Are guarding the slumbering world,
My fancy creates me visions of yore,
  That ravish my heart with their spell,
And, happy, I dream the sexton, once more,
  Is ringing that resonant bell.
    O, hallowed Church, so dear,
How often, at eve, I fancy thy songs resound,
    And invoke the scenes, long fled,
    And recall the friends, long dead,
And summon the days when childhood, with joy.
                                    was crown'd.

I have roved thro' groves of olive and palm,
  And trespassed on Arctic's domain;
The ocean I've sailed, in tempest and calm,
  And sauntered thro' temple and fane;

And often I've stood where worshipers thronged,
　As music through corridors rolled,
Yet ever, 'mid all, I strangely have longed,
　That ruin to sadly behold.
　　O, hallowed Church, so dear,
The echoing notes of anthems, so rich, so clear,
　　And of chants, so full, so sure,
　　And of hymns, so soft, so pure,
I'm longing to hear awaken thy walls, so drear.

AN ‌IRISHMAN.

Be there a sad note
  In an Irishman's lays,
Yet joy will be found
  In his rhythmical line;
And be there a cloud,
  Over all of his days,
He gladdens the rifts
  With effulgence divine.

Inyan Kara.[8]

O Thou, my Inyan Kara,
  Thou Mount, in mount's embrace,
No more by Arla-Eeka,
  My steps to thee I trace;
O Thou, where merry songsters
  Sent echoes far and wide,
And gave a wildwood greeting
  To her, my dusky bride.

O Thou, my Inyan Kara,
  Thou Mount, with breath of bloom,
No more, by Arla-Eeka,
  I scent thy rare perfume;
O Thou, where oft I wandered,
  With light and wary tread,
To find, amid thy windings,
  The haunt where prey had fled.

O Thou, my Inyan Kara,
   Thou Mount, of rugged height,
No more, by Arla-Eeka,
   I watch the eagles' flight;
O Thou, where morning greeting
   I gave to rising sun,
Then knelt to distant altar,
   Where hero rites were done.

O Thou, my Inyan Kara,
   Thou Mount, from earth's unrest,
My own, my Arla-Eeka,
   Now sleeps upon thy breast;
O Thou, where fallen chieftain
   Is rocked by forest arms,
While Zephyr croons above him,
   And stills the Wind's alarms.

O Thou, my Inyan Kara,
   Thou Mount, from vanished sea,
To meet my Arla-Eeka,
   In dreams I fly to thee;
O Thou, where ne'er I'll wander,
   To list to plaintive pine,
Nor scale thy sunlit summit,
   To kneel to warrior shrine.

Oh, I often dream
    Of the happy, happy golden hours,
        Whiled away,
            Gaily whiled away,
When, with romping ones,
    Seeking dainty, dainty, fairy flow'rs,
        I would stray,
            Idly I would stray;
And, with glee untold,
    Caroled many, many, simple songs,
        Childish songs,
            Simple, childish songs;—

Ah, those joys of old,
　　Come in wooing, wooing, cheering throngs,
　　　　While I dream,
　　　　　　While I sweetly dream.

Oh, I often dream,
　　As the lurking, lurking imps of care,
　　　　Haunt my way,
　　　　　　Grimly haunt my way,
Of the darling ones,
　　Who my heavy, heavy trials share,
　　　　Day by day,
　　　　　　Kindly, day by day;
Then a hand above,
　　Conquers ev'ry, ev'ry lurking foe,
　　　　Haunting foe,
　　　　　　Lurking, haunting foe,
And the rays of love,
　　Make my dreary, dreary pathway glow,

While I dream,
  While I sweetly dream.

Oh, I often dream
  Of the final, final end of strife,
    Soon to be,
      Very soon to be,
When the shining ones,
  Thro' the blessed, blessed gates of life,
    Come for me,
      Gladly come for me;
Then, where none repine,
  I will ever, ever surely dwell,
    Safely dwell,
      Surely, safely dwell,
And, with bliss divine,
  Hear the holy, holy anthems swell,
    While I dream,
      While I sweetly dream.

Field of Life.

The world is a field, where trials abound,
And errors are met, and evils are found;
And soldiers of Right, must ever be strong,
In smiting to earth, the vassals of Wrong.

The valiant alone, may victories win,
In fighting the hosts of treacherous sin,
As faltering arm ne'er parries a blow,
Nor craven of heart, ne'er conquers a foe.

But when we have fought and victories won,
And all of our deeds are worthily done,
The Father divine, will give as a prize,
A beautiful home where Joy never dies.

And then, from the throne of jasper and gold,
The good we have done, will gladly be told;
And all of the love, we've planted in gloom,
Will blossom in light, and evermore bloom.

What Is Man?

An Alchemist,
Who wields the wonder-working stone;
A Worshiper,
Who meekly bows at Mammon's throne;
A Monarchist,
Who basely wills that gold should reign;
A Laborer,
Who meanly dies the slave of Gain.

The Bern Minster.

High Mass of the Muses."

IN careless mood, I chanced to roam,
Near wonderland's majestic dome,
That long had stood, a soldier stern,
To ward the sons of storied Berne.

The sun had gone to dreamful rest,
Behind a silvered mountain-crest;
And balmy eve, with smile serene,
Had gently veiled the valleys green.

'Twas then the time, as darkness grew,
And verdure quaffed the nectar dew,
That many sought that stately pile,
An idle hour to there beguile.

While yet I roamed, the minster bell
Sent forth, afar, o'er mount and dell,
A voice that strangely seemed to say:
The Muses hold High Mass to-day.

And then, tho' faint the light had grown,
I marked that poem, wrought in stone,
Whose tower low, seemed ill, a part
Of that rare mold of gothic art.

Ere yet the bell had ceased to woo,
And o'er the crags had tongued "adieu,"
I paused to note, then joined the tide,
That drifted thro' the entrance wide.

No flaming jets, with dazzling glare,
Then welcomed those who gathered there,
But feeble tapers gleamed on high,
Like twinkling lights in vaulted sky.

The Muses famed, those mystic maids,
Then wandered thro' the ghostly shades,
And sung a simple, winning song,
That held entranced, the list'ning throng.

And e'en as yet the maidens sang,
A herald call of triumph, rang,
And martial strains re-echoed then,
Like bugle notes in Alpine glen.

But soon there came an angry jar,
That seemed to come from tempest car,
And then a storm, in fury, broke,
With clash and clang of cymbal stroke.

The god of winds, unloosed the breeze,
And hidden hands swept magic keys,
While brazen mouths gave startling blare,
And wizard notes seemed everywhere.

Then bassoons laughed and viols sighed,
And trombones sobbed and hautboys cried,
And clarinets, with voices shrill,
Repeating, mocked the flute's soft trill.

As e'en I list, in half day-dream,
Methought I heard a purling stream,
And zephyrs, whisp'ring o'er the leas,
And songsters, warbling in the trees.

Methought I roved in sylvan bow'rs,
Amid the fragrant, fairy flow'rs,
While harp and lute and ancient lyre,
Made music sweet as siren choir.

Still, o'er the sounds, so weird, so wild,
The Muses' song came soft and mild,
And yet, in tone, so rich, so clear,
'Twas off'ring fit for angel's ear.

And yet the witching song went on,
Till other sounds were hushed and gone,
And then, tho' mourned by fond Delight,
Its spirit winged its upward flight.

Thus closed the song:
                              "All hail, to thee,
Apollo, thou god of harmony;
Thou dwellest apart in shady nooks,
Where revel the fays and babbling brooks;
Thou knowest the notes of heav'n and earth,
For, Patron, 'twas thou who gave them birth.

Thou tunest our harps on sacred mount,
And quenchest our thirst at inspired fount;
Thou guidest our feet where'er we go,
And ever we joy thy will to know;
So, whither we roam, we sing to thee,
Apollo, thou god of harmony."

When Maidens' voice had ceased to ring,
And restful night had spread her wing,
Each one went forth with rapture filled,
Who whiled that hour. where music thrilled.

For fifty years, a monarch there,
Had ruled, with song, that haunt of pray'r;
And hearts that came in earthly chains,
He quickly freed with heav'nly strains.

And all those sounds — of lyre, of lute,
Of breeze, of brook, of harp, of flute,
Of song, of storm, of warblers' trill —
Were organ-notes, made by his skill.

Then wreath of renown,
From earth,
We bring,

And chant, while we crown,
    With worth,
        The King:
O, long be thy days,
    Thy heart still young!
O, sweet be thy lays,
    Thy harp unstrung!
Thou King of the soul,
    Thro' chords divine,
May strains ever roll,
    With thrall like thine.

Tho' the world is abloom,
In the heart there is gloom,
And lips of gladness are dumb,
    For the land of the brave,
    Is a prey to the knave,
Who murders his brother with rum.

By the bright, sunny way,
Where the youth are at play,
There dwells, in splendor, a foe,
    That allures and beguiles,
    And depraves and defiles,
And revels in visions of woe.

In the thrill of the wine,
And the spell of the vine,
There seems no sorrow nor care,
But the dregs of the bowl,
Are the tears of the soul,
Awakened by frenzied despair.

Let us strike with a will,
At the hosts of the still,
Let us strike, for the foe is at hand,
And delight will resound,
For the right will be crowned,
And beauty will garland the land.

A Suffragist Sufferer.

Ach, frau, mein frau, mein liebe frau,
Such dricks, as dese, I don't allow;
You go so soon, und sthay so late,
Unt makes poor Fritz for supper vait;
Unt neffer makes de fires no more,
Nor chops de woot, like once pefore;
Unt say, vat use hab men for fraus,
Ven dey, demselves, must milk de cows?
Ach, donner, how I hates dose men,
Dat gomes here dwenty dimes again,
Unt dakes you off pefore mein eyes,
No madder how dot paby cries;
Unt, frau, I dells you vat I says:
Iv you don't sthop dose horrit vays,
I'll for dose fellers chust will lie,
Unt gick meinself unt plack mein eye,
Unt den yourself gone det you'll see,
Veil hanging on von hazel dree.

The Trio of sirens were queens of the sea,
That conquer'd the waters by rugged Capri;
Then govern'd their kingdom, so famous and strong,
Thro' power of magic—the magic of song.

Those consorts of Pluto, were fair to behold;
Their ebon-hued tresses were fretted with gold;
Their innocent faces were haloed with light;
Their heavenly glances put darkness to flight.

Their words were as winning as angel e'er spoke;
Their notes were as thrilling as goddess e'er woke;
Their tones were so wooing that none ever tried
To pass by unheeding — all hearkened and died.

Those mystical maidens, with only a breath,
The fearless and mighty deliver'd to death;
They smilingly fettered the noble and proud,
Then gave the enchanted a billowy shroud.

The homeward-bound sailor, who paused on his oar,
To hear their sweet voices, ne'er gained the lov'd shore;
The hero, whose prowess had won the world's praise,
To Lethe they wafted by beautiful lays.

Those queens so beguiling, allured to destroy;
Their wands were of upas, to slay was their joy;
Their coral-paved kingdom was only a grave
That cruelly welcomed the victim they gave.

Those sirens accursed, now govern no more,
They, too, are sepulchred where surging waves roar;
Tho' sisters, more cruel, their flags have unfurl'd
To conquer and ruin a perishing world.

Those others are Avarice, Envy and Hate,—
The one, a grim tyrant, no power can sate,
The second, a dragon, the parent of woe,
The other, a demon, a murderous foe.

The hand of the tyrant e'er crushes the heart;
The tongue of the dragon is Satan's own dart;
The fangs of the demon give quickly and sure
The wound that no Mercy nor Pardon can cure.

Those rulers e'er offer, with scoffing and sneers,
To sorrowing mortals, a goblet of tears;
They wither the flowers that bloom in the soul;
They madden and anguish, to damn is their goal.

HOPE'S OFFERING.

Set free from sin's beguiling snare,
Set free from loads of grinding care,
Set free from bonds of grim despair,
  We shall true pleasure share.

Above the depths where troubles flow,
Above the plains where sorrows grow,
Above the heights of somber woe,
  We shall of heaven know.

Beside the waters, cool and sweet,
Beside the throne where loved ones meet,
Beside the dear-bought mercy-seat,
  We shall the Savior greet.

LAND OF REST.

BLESSED Realm,
  Where all may be,
With eye of faith,
  We look to thee;
O, smiling Land,
  Of holy throngs,
With ear of hope,
  We hear thy songs;
O, heav'nly Home,
  A message blest,
Invites to thee —
  The Land of Rest.

I wandered in the northland,
  Where lakes, enchanting, slept,
While o'er the day expiring,
  The eve, in silence, wept;
And as the starry soldiers
  Came forth to guard the sky,

I heard a voice repeating
  The strange and truthful cry:
    Only a fool I see,
    A fool, a fool I see!—
    Thus sung the loon to me,
    The loony loon to me.

And as that cry re-echoed,
  I thought of ladies fair,
Of those with powdered faces,
  Who spoil their lovely hair,
And lace themselves so tightly,
  They can but barely sigh;—
Poor things, they, too, should listen,
  And hear the truthful cry:
    Only a fool I see,
    A fool, a fool I see!—
    Thus sung the loon to thee,
    The loony loon to thee.

And then I thought of others,
  Of youths with slender canes,
Who smoke cigars so proudly,
  And wear such massive chains,
And stand upon the corners,
  To see the girls go by;—
Poor things, they, too, should listen,
  And hear the truthful cry:
    Only a fool I see,
    A fool, a fool I see!—
    Thus sung the loon to thee,
    The loony loon to thee.

And then I thought of others,
  Of those with wealth untold,
Who sell their souls for money,
  And worship only gold;
Who have no tears for sorrow,
  And wipe no weeping eye;—

Poor things, they, too, should listen,
  And hear the truthful cry:
    Only a fool I see,
    A fool, a fool I see!—
    Thus sung the loon to thee,
    The loony loon to thee.

And then I thought of others,
  Of those with hopes of fame,
Who seem to think that honor
  May come thro' sin and shame;
Who basely bribe the voter,
  And God and man defy;—
Poor things, they, too, should listen,
  And hear the truthful cry:
    Only a fool I see,
    A fool, a fool I see!—
    Thus sung the loon to thee,
    The loony loon to thee.

Ah well, we all, insanely,
  Go rushing on thro' life,
Pursuing fleeting pleasure,
  Thro' days and years of strife;
But ere we grasp the phantom,
  We stumble, fall and die; —
Poor things, we all should listen,
  And hear the truthful cry:
    Only a fool I see,
    A fool, a fool I see! —
    Thus sung the loon to me,
    The loony loon to thee.

When night has veiled the earth, so fair,
    And hosts of heaven are guarding the land,
The boy repeats his ev'ning prayer,
    Then says: Dear Mamma, O give me your hand.

And when his youthful days are done,
    Tho' proud and stately, no ruler more grand,
He yields the heart to some fair one,
    And pleads: My Idol, O give me your hand.

And when, to him, the world is drear,
   And waves of sorrow, break over life's strand,
He seeks, at home, for words of cheer,
   And sighs: My Darling, O give me your hand.

And when, the cares of life are o'er,
   And round him, weeping, the loving ones stand,
He bids his friends to grieve no more,
   Then prays: Dear Father, O give me Your Hand.

The Father Seeth All.

In the days when we are building
  Stately castles in the air,
And when youthful joys enrapture,
  And no clouds are seen of care,
We should heed the voice of heaven,
  Ere the sins of earth enthrall,
And, thro' life, fore'er remember
  That the Father seeth all.

And when time has borne us onward,
  To the fields of ripened age,
Where the mighty hosts are gathered,
  And for food the battle wage,
And where few may fill their garners,
  While the rest for succor call,
We should surely then remember
  That the Father seeth all.

Should we safely ride the waters,
  While the foamy billows rave,
And neglect to pause for others,
  Who are wrecked upon the wave,
When we near the icy ocean,
  On whose bosom floats the pall,
We will sadly then remember
  That the Father seeth all.

And at last, when toil is over,
  And we've crossed the vale of years,
If for others we have labored,
  And have helped to dry their tears,
Tho' the sweets our lips have tasted,
  May have seemed to turn to gall,
We will gladly then remember
  That the Father seeth all.

THE UNFAILING CRUSE.

When thy cares are pressing,
And when joy withholds its blessing,
Should some one be weeping,
O'er the hopes behind him sleeping,
Dry the tears then welling,
Kindly all his grief dispelling,
And thy act, so holy,
Will make light thy heart, so lowly.

A THIRTY YEARS' DREAM.[1]

Where is that little school-house, Alf,
   That stood beside the lane?
I looked for it to-day, but, strange,
   I looked for it in vain;
It may have been I could not see,
   For something made me weep,
But if I saw, then I have had
   A Rip Van Winkle sleep.

We were but school-boys yesterday —
   At least, to me, it seems
As if a single fleeting night
   Now dims our boyhood dreams;
Then why say you that we're not young?
   You know you can't be right,
For boys don't grow to bearded men,
   At once, in one short night.

Ah, Alf, what splendid times we've had
    Within that school house old!
We there have played most roguish tricks —
    The half were never told!
Each object in that humble room,
    We've hallow'd with our sins; —
You know, last week the teacher sat
    Upon some crooked pins.

We've marred the desks and notched the seats
    With jack-knives sharp and bright,
And cuffed our books and scratched our slates,
    As school-boys have the right;
And if it chanced that now and then,
    The teacher boxed our ears,
We scarcely cared, for joy was nigh
    To kiss away our tears.

At twelve o'clock — that blessed hour,
    When time for play begun
We sallied forth with bounding hearts,
    Intent on having fun;
At times we sought the woods near by,
    To plague the wary squirrels,
At other times, we loitered round
    To plague the chary girls.

The fort we built, not long ago,
    Was strong and finely planned,
And those brave lads who stormed it, Alf,
    Declared it was well manned;
For tho' they far outnumbered us,
    We yet fought long and well,
But when our balls of snow gave out,
    Of course our colors fell.

Last week we helped the girls to build
   Their play-house all anew;
Then furnished it with mossy seats,
   And soft, green carpets, too;
And made a cupboard with one shelf,
   To hold their china-ware;—
Don't you suppose, when we are gone
   A fairy queen lives there?

When yesterday, our school was out,
  I bounded thro' the door
Of that old house, with gladsome shout,
  Nor cared to see it more;
And then, at nine, I went to bed,
  With heart all filled with joy,
For mother's voice had softly said:
  Good night, my darling boy!

And then I heard a gentle song —
  "Lie still, my child, and sleep!"
But soon the song seemed more a prayer—
  "May heav'n thy footsteps keep!"
And then I dreamed a troubled dream,
  Of fancies strange and wild;
I thought I ceased, at once, to be
  A laughing, romping child.

I dreamed I moved away out West—
  As oft I've longed to do—
And met and loved a schoolma'm there,
  And wooed and won her too;
And then I thought a girl and boy
  Came climbing on my knee,
And, strange to say, my friends declared
  Those children looked like me.

And then my fancy bore me on,
  O'er many a stranger land;
It carried me o'er ocean waves,
  . O'er vales and mountains grand;
And ere I turned my rambling feet,
  To take the homeward way,
I thought the icy breath of age,
  Had tinged my hair with gray.

When I awoke, I felt so worn,
  I could not help but cry;
And schooltime, Alf, still found me sad—
  I really can't tell why!
And then I went, with heavy heart,
  To meet my comrades dear,
And found that e'en the house was gone,
  And not a soul came near.

And as, perplexed, I waited there,
  The cars went thund'ring o'er
The very grounds on which we played
  A single night before.—
Now tell me, Alf, how comes all this?
  Who took the house away?
What has become of all the boys?
  Where are the girls to day?

          *   *   *

Alas, say you my dream was true,
  And that our youth has fled?
That all the boys and girls are gone,
  Or rest among the dead?
Then, truly, Alf, I've sweetly dreamed
  A score of years and ten;—
O, would that I could dream for aye,
  That we were boys again.

Do Not Fear.

Fainting one, on foamy sea,
Reaching out its arms for thee,
Do not fear the angry wave,
For a Friend thy bark will save.

Dreary one, in desert lone,
List'ning to the wind's sad moan,
Do not fear, tho' bleak the sky,
For a Friend is standing nigh.

Weary one, in depths of woe,
Wand'ring as the shadows grow,
Do not fear the gath'ring night,
For a Friend will give thee light.

When the cheeks of morn are glowing,
  None may bid the blush be gone,
And when eyes of eve are paling,
  None may bid the light stream on;
So, when Love comes stealing coyly,
  None may frown the sprite away,
And, when Love would play the truant,
  None may coax the rogue to stay.

The Voice of Hope.

O, Care, while hearts before you are bending,
   The Voice of Hope its message is sending,
To flood dull eyes with visions of beauty,
   And nerve the arm by challenge to duty.

O, Want, while gloom about you is falling,
   The Voice of Hope is tenderly calling,
To drive the clouds from hearts of the dreary,
   And woo the dreams that strengthen the weary.

O, Grief, while tears are telling your sadness,
  The Voice of Hope sends radiant gladness,
To hush the moans of murmuring sorrow,
  And blush the now with rays of the morrow.

O, Woe, while mounds beneath you are springing,
  The Voice of Hope is soothingly ringing,
To lift the soul where joys are unending,
  And loves of earth, in oneness, are blending.

O, Voice, rejoice and echo forever,
  To thrill the will with dauntless endeavor;
And sing and wing the beautiful story,
  That still shall fill the world with new glory.

JOYLESS YOUTH.

I feel quite sure the children now,
 Know naught of childish joys,
For I ne'er see a girlish girl,
 Nor hear of boyish boys;
Indeed, they look so very odd,
 I fancy they are elves,
That chase the darkness from our skies,
 Yet live in gloom themselves.

In summer time, the lads incase
 Their feet in useless shoes —
As wise 'twould be to shield the grass
 From God's refreshing dews;
And then they are so richly clad,
 And do not care to romp,
Not knowing that an hour of joy,
 Outweighs an age of pomp.

We used to call the little maids
  Forget-me-nots, so dear,
But girls are now like jewel-weeds,
  Those touch-me-nots, so queer;
For foolish fashion decks them out,
  In jewels, silks and lace,
And gives to them a jaunty look,
  But ne'er a lovely face.

In dear old times, our parents said,
  If we could write and read,
And cipher thro' the rule of three,
  'Twas all we e'er would need;
The brain was ne'er o'erburdened then,
  The youthful heart was light;
The cheek by blushing health was kissed,
  The eye with joy was bright.

It was with digits we were taught
    To reckon, when at school,
But now it seems that wiser heads
    Have wrought a wiser rule;
For when, last week, I chanced to go
    To school, on closing day,
I saw a scholar working sums
    In some new-fashioned way.

Thus, he declared and said he proved
    That a, b, minus c,
Just equaled d, plus e, f square,
    When multiplied by g;
Of course his words were wondrous wise,
    Of that I had no doubt,
But why and how he figured so,
    I failed to figure out.

A while I watched his thoughtful face,
  And marked his languid looks,
Then said, " A problem solve for me,
  Not found within the books;
You seem to know life's value, lad,
  Plus study, minus mirth;
Now, if, to study, mirth you add,
  Then what would life be worth ? "

The young folks have no time to-day,
  For sport or childish dreams;
Their only pastime seems to be
  To sail on classic streams;
For now they reap from modern fields,
  And glean from ancient lore,
And feast their minds, on choicest fruits,
  Till brain will hold no more.

The boldest heights that Thought has reared,
   They now attempt to scale,
With far more zeal than chastened knight
   E'er sought the Holy Grail;
In short, they give with lavish hand,
   The food to feed the flame,
That glows within the lamp, by which
   Man finds his way to fame.

Altho' 'tis true that knowledge lights
   The road to honors great,
And tho' the wise are best prepared
   To break the lance with fate,
The youths who strive to win renown,
   But take no time for play,
Will weary soon and fail at last,
   To bear the prize away.

Across a smiling sea,
  In rosy morn of spring,
Hope gently came to me,
  On light and silv'ry wing,
And with her mystic wand,
  Entranced the bending skies,
And, in the bright beyond,
  Made spendid visions rise;—
  Visions rise, joylit skies.

And then my fancy flew,
  O'er wide and wooing plains,
While huts to castles grew,
  And fields to vast domains;
And hand of siren fame,
  With glory robed my days,
And nations gave acclaim,
  And sung me songs of praise;—
  Songs of praise, witching days.

Ere long the vision fled,
  Beyond a shoreless wave,
And round me grief was spread,
  And near me yawned a grave,
While earth itself grew drear,
  And face of nature paled,
And, o'er the fading year,
  The notes of autumn wailed;—
  Autumn wailed, loved ones paled.

But soon across the sea,
　Across the dreamy deep,
Hope winged again to me,
　Her plighted troth to keep,
And with her fairy wand,
　Swung back the gates of gloom,
And morn eternal dawned,
　Above a vanquished tomb;--
　Vanquished tomb, vanished gloom.

The Curlew Song.

I ROVED in western wonder-land,
    Enraptured by a vision grand,
Where wand of God, in age unknown,
Had swayed across an ocean zone,
And changed a vast and mighty deep
To boundless fields where millions reap;
   And where the bird, with carol sweet,
   And plumage bright and pinion fleet,
   Flew gaily on, its love to greet;
And while I roved, a curlew, coy,
With breast of gold and heart of joy,

Swept on before, and sung and sang
The happy song, that rung and rang:
   I bathe my wing in pearly dew,
   And sing and sing, dear mate, for you;
   I cleave the air when foe is nigh,
   Nor care, nor care, dear mate, have I.

I stood within the world of trade,
And marked the cares by riches made;
I saw its dupes, in surging street,
Pursuing wealth, with aching feet;
I saw it drive them madly on,
Tho' weary day to rest had gone;
   And then I heard desponding sighs,
   And marked how few had won the prize,
   And saw how wretched miser dies;
And then I thought: What slaves they are!
To be like them?—'twere better far,

To be the bird that sung and sang
The happy song that rung and rang:
  I bathe my wing in pearly dew,
  And sing and sing, dear mate, for you;
  I cleave the air when foe is nigh,
  Nor care, nor care, dear mate, have I.

I strolled thro' stately, gilded halls,
And marked the ways in siren balls;
I saw, within the mazy dance,
The eye of beauty hotly glance;
I saw the cheek of manhood glow,
Inspired by wine and passions low;
  And then I heard a tale of woe,
  And marked a reeling drunkard go,
  And saw a wanton, wicked blow;
And then I thought: What knaves they are!
To be like them?—'twere better far,

To be the bird that sung and sang
The happy song that rung and rang:
   I bathe my wing in pearly dew,
   And sing and sing, dear mate, for you;
   I cleave the air when foe is nigh,
   Nor care, nor care, dear mate, have I.

And then I roamed 'mid real worth,
And marked the scenes where joy has birth;
I saw the laughing eye of youth,
Reflect the light of holy truth;
I saw the eve of life come on,
And bring a hope of golden dawn;
   And then I heard the voice of song,
   And marked a land unruled by wrong,
   And saw a glad, contented throng;
And then I thought: How wise they are!
To be like them were better far,

Than be the bird that sung and sang
The happy song, that rung and rang:
  I bathe my wing in pearly dew,
  And sing, and sing, dear mate, for you;
  I cleave the air when foe is nigh,
  Nor care, nor care, dear mate, have I.

SAILING 'NEATH THE CROSS.

When you leave the harbor, in the glow of morning,
  Thinking not of danger, dreaming not of loss,
Hear you then the Master give the gentle warning:
  Sailor, make thy voyage, sailing 'neath the cross.

When you ride the ocean, storms around you beating,
  Battling with the billows, that in fury toss,
Hear you then the Master lovingly entreating:
  Sailor, seek for safety, sailing 'neath the cross,

When you sight the haven, with a joy enthralling,
  Bringing golden treasure, unalloyed by dross,
Hear you then the Master, o'er the waters, calling:
  Sailor, speed thy nearing, sailing 'neath the cross.

I'LL SING.

I'll sing in the morning
  A song to the King,
Whose magic awakened
  The slumbering spring;
Whose fiat has given
  The streamlets their birth,
Whose pencil is painting
  The flowers of earth.

I'll sing in the morning
  A song to the One,
Whose splendor is mirrored
  In dewdrop and sun;
Whose smiling is answered
  By mountain and plain,
Whose glory is murmured
  By billows of grain.

I'll sing in the morning
 A song to the Lord,
Whose bounty has given
 The reapers reward;
Whose fountains have flooded
 The meadows with gold,
Whose goodness and mercy
 Can never be told.

I'll sing in the morning
 A song to the Guide,
Whose mandate can silence
 The tempest and tide;
Whose presence is sunlight
 In winter and gloom,
Whose pleasure makes Eden
 Eternally bloom.

I'll praise The Redeemer,
  In days of the spring,
And praise Him in summer,
  When boughs gently swing,
And praise Him in autumn,
  When leaves are a-wing,
And praise Him in winter,—
  Yes, ever I'll sing.

With tireless tread, Pandora goes,
And bears, with pride, the box of woes
She brought, to earth, to give the one
Who mocked the gods and robbed the sun.

That dowry gift supplies her well,
With human hurts—those imps of hell;
And so she wends thro' ev'ry land,
And deals out ills with lavish hand.

She finds her way to hut and hall,
And flings a tear to great and small;
And e'en as buds by frosts are killed,
So hearts, of love, by her are stilled.

And yet within her box of pain,
Of hope, there lies one golden grain,
And he to whom she gives a woe,
May find the gem concealed below.

And he who gains that golden gift,
In sorrow's cloud will see the rift;
And tho' he treads the vale of gloom,
Will scent the rose of rare perfume.

O, thankless one, then thankful be,
Nor scorn the grief she brings to thee;
For tho' she wounds thy tender heart,
She offers balm to cure the smart.

BAIT.

In the streams of life
  that swiftly glide,
Where the hooks are cast
  for honors great,
Tho' the few may land
  the game with pride,
All the rest of earth
  must cut the bait.

For the one who holds the potent reel
  O'er the depths that bear our ship of state,
Has a need no more to bless the keel
  Than he has the friends who cut the bait.

So, the ones who seek for miser gold,
  In the wake of fears and dogged by hate,
Gather up and hoard their wealth untold,
  By the toil of those who cut the bait.

And the ones who own the flying trains,
  That are borne on wings of seeming fate,
Hurry on the wheels, thro' snows and rains,
  By the skill of those who cut the bait.

But the man who gains the final goal,
  Where the wreaths of fame for victor wait,
Very soon has learned to wield the pole
  With a hand that knows to cut the bait.

Content.

Where the fowl, with a lordly pride,
　Calls to the drowsy morn,
And the pig, with a careless stride,
　Roams in a wealth of corn,
And the cow, in the twilight wan,
　Rests in the narrow lane,
And the horse, at the blush of dawn,
　Feeds in the boundless plain,
Remote from the fields of strife,
And sweet from the Fount of life,
Content, with the grace of rhyme,
Flows o'er the sands of time.

Where the lad, by the limpid brook,
  Sits with a rural rod,
And the dog, in a restful nook,
  Sleeps on the velvet sod,
And the lark, with a liquid trill,
  Mounts to the bending sky,
And the breeze, with a mystic thrill,
  Makes to the bird reply,
Remote from the
              fields of strife,
And glad from
          the Source of life,
Content, with
          a bliss divine,
Bows at
    a sylvan
        shrine.

Where the light, on a peaceful scene,
　Falls where the zephyrs play,
And the wood, with a smile serene,
　Lies in the arms of day,
And the bud, with the rifting crown,
　Swells to the gorgeous rose,
And the eve, in a silvered gown,
　Sinks to a soft repose,
Remote from the
　　　fields of strife
And bright from
　　　the Throne
　　　　　of life,
Content, with
　　　a wizard hand,
Rules o'er the
　　　love-lit land

KITTY.

Ah, my pet, so sweetly sleeping,
While the phantom shades are creeping,
Wake at once, for now I'm lonely,
But for you am longing only;—
     Wake, my Kitty, wake.

Ah, my pet,
     so gently waking,
Come to me, your rug
     forsaking,
And my arms shall safely rest you,
Where no one will dare molest you;—
     Come, my Kitty, come.

Ah, my pet, so softly purring,
Even tho' the mice are stirring,
Sing to me, nor heed their scheming,
Even tho' they think you dreaming;—
    Sing, my Kitty, sing.

WHAT?

What hope is yours, O one with darling boy?
What dream is yours, that fills your soul with joy?
What path is that, you counsel him to tread?
What pray'r is that, you whisper o'er his bed?
    A hope that Worth will crown his name;
    A dream that Time will sing his fame;
    A path that sin has ne'er defiled;
    A pray'r for grace for him, my child.

What hope is yours, O fond and trusting lad?
What dream is yours, that makes your heart so glad?
What path is that, you vow you e'er will keep?
What pray'r is that, you say before you sleep?
    A hope that cheers like meed of praise;
    A dream that Right will guide my ways;
    A path that leads to heights above;
    A pray'r that sweeps the chords of love.

What now the hope, O worn and faithful one?
What now the dream for him, your wayward son?
What now the path he goes with falt'ring pace?
What now the pray'r for him, who sneers at grace?
    A hope that ends in grief and gloom;
    A dream that tells of death and doom;
    A path where Furies rove and rave;
    A pray'r, to God, for help to save.

What now the hope, O man of golden dawn?
What now the dream to spur and woo you on?
What now the path that yet before you lies?
What now the pray'r you send to greet the skies?
    A hope an imp would dread to claim;
    A dream of woe and want and shame;
    A path where serpents writhe and crawl;
    A pray'r for drink, a curse, is all.

HAVE I THY LOVE.

I may claim thy love alone,
  For trust I will not pine,
As love is but the bud alone,
  That bursts to trust divine;
Then shield the bud of love from cold,
So that, to full, it may unfold:
Yes, ever guard, with tender care,
The bud that bursts to bloom so rare,
    If with, or without trust.

Tho' free from trust, pure love alone,
  Has often pleased and won,
But free from love, sure trust alone,
  Has charmed and conquered none;
Then shield the bud of love from cold,
So that, to full, it may unfold;
Yes, ever guard, with tender care,
The bud that bursts to bloom so rare,
    If with, or without trust.

Old Mammon is the mighty king,
Whom mortals serve and nations sing,
And yet who sneers at friend and foe,
And grimly smiles at want and woe.

The king is he, whose cruel reign
Has taught the heart to bow to brain;
And who now breaks, on rack of greed,
The ones that yield him servile heed.

Ay, he's the wretch who takes the boys,
And robs them of their childhood joys,
Then goads them on like galley slaves
And scourges them to early graves.

And he's the one, of miser hand,
Who gathers wealth in ev'ry land,
And crushes love beneath his heels,
Nor e'en one pang of pity feels.

Ah, he's the king, of crimes untold,
Who damns his folk with curse of gold,
And ne'er a deed, of worth, has done,
Nor paid the meed that Worth has won.

And e'er he rules the vassal world,
And keeps a pirate flag unfurled,
And even holds despotic sway,
When Rest would claim her precious day.

Then down with him, the sordid one,
Who basely plans, from sun to sun,
To frighten sleep from teary eyes,
And fill the earth with weary sighs.

The Voyage.

HO, ho! we slip the hawser,
    And loose, and launch the boat,
To speed upon the waters,
    To joy, to dream and float;
For Fancy sends but pleasure,
    To cleave, to breast the deep,
Where waves seem molten silver,
    Becalmed, bewitched to sleep.

Heigho! upon life's ocean,
  We race, we glide along,
And hail the pulsing billows,
  With laugh, with shout and song;
For wings of snowy canvas,
  Have kissed, have caught the breeze,
And bear us swiftly onward,
  To sing, to rule the seas.

But lo! we're sadly longing
  To greet, to gain the shore,
For billows now are foaming,
  And leap, and toss and roar,
And giant winds are wailing
  A threat, a dirge of woe,
And mighty depths are calling
  To beds, to graves below.

But no! the winds have vanished,
  To rave, to wail no more,
And ocean-waves have banished
  The frown, the scowl they wore,
And all we weary **farers**
  In port, in peace may **be,**
Where tempests do not gather,
  To lash, to rouse the sea.

We're on life's ocean sailing,
  Sailing day by day,
And o'er the billows bounding,
  Bounding far away,
And tho' the waters thunder,
  Thunder 'neath the gale,
We yet may voyage safely,
  Safely home may sail.

The Present truly seems unjust,
   For oft it pays where naught is due,
And then again lays claim to trust,
   From those who've rendered service true.

It fawns on those of princely birth,
   And smooths the sunny paths they tread,
And surfeits them on fat of earth,
   While Merit dines on crusts of bread.

But tho' it bows to royal will,
   And lowly bends at gilded shrine,
It scorns the one whose magic skill
   Enchants the world with chords divine:

Who sweetly sings on sacred mount,
   And stirs the pulse of Rapture there,
And gladly fills, at fabled fount,
   The cup of Joy for lips of Care.

Who gladdens poor as well as rich,
   For cottage writes as well as hall,
And wakens notes, that woo and witch
   Alike in dance and courtly ball.

Whose song is like the dainty bloom,
   That bursts beside the dusty road,
And floods the air with rich perfume,
   For all who bear life's heavy load.

And yet, altho' he lifts the cloud,
   That darkly veils the face of day,
There swell, for him, no plaudits loud,
   Nor twines, for him, a wreath of bay.

But tho' the Present thus is dumb,
　　When Right demands that praise should ring,
In time, to be, Delight will come,
　　And o'er the tomb of Merit sing.

The Present spreads o'er titled dead,
　　A purple pall of richest woof,
And makes for him a marble bed,
　　Beneath the mausoleum's roof.

But when the artist lays him down —
　　His couch perchance a pauper bier —
The Present dons no sable gown,
　　Nor deigns to shed a kindly tear.

And yet, when kingly vault is locked,
　　The key is thrown in Lethe's wave;
And loving Thought has rarely knocked,
　　Where slumber those in royal grave.

But great composers never die,
　E'en tho' their earthly race be run;
For whereso'er they live or lie,
　There is, for them, no setting sun.

And polished stone may claim no part,
　When artist wears the crown of fame;
For then, within the human heart,
　The hand of God has graved his name.

Only a few little rays of dawn,
　　Giving a glimmer of light;
Only a smile, and the day is gone,
　　Leaving the shadows of night;
So, gladly we cling to the hand above,
And carol a song of the morn of love.

Only a few little strands of fate,
　　Given to mortals to spin;
Only a step to the mystic gate,
　　Swinging its welcoming-in;
So, gladly we go at the day's decline,
To revel in bliss, in a realm divine.

Only a few little days are ours,
    Laden with labor and strife;
Only a few little wayside flow'rs,
    Blossom in valleys of life;
So, gladly we press thro' the vales of gloom,
To beautiful fields in the land of bloom.

WHEN?

When baby receives the fatherly kiss,
When little ones coo, in heavenly bliss,
When parent and child sing hallowed lays,
When rapture resounds in lowliest ways,
   O Sot, O Thou, of smouldering brain,
   Do sights, like these, give pleasure or pain?
   O Sot, O Thou, of darkening sky,
   Do sights, like these, awaken no sigh?

When motherly love gives happiness birth,
When little ones shout their innocent mirth,
When parlor is strewn with trinkets and toys,
When orchard is filled with frolicking boys,
   O Sot, O Thou, of smouldering brain,
   Do sights, like these, give pleasure or pain?
   O Sot, O Thou, of withering heart,
   Do sights, like these, awaken no smart?

When Evil entraps the manliest men,
When Virtue is lost in hideous den,
When Furies dethrone the goddess of Right,
When Horrors invoke the demons of night,
  O Sot, O Thou, of smouldering brain,
  Do sights, like these, give pleasure or pain?
  O Sot, O Thou of perishing soul,
  Do sights, like these, betoken a goal?

When shivering wife is flying with dread,
When hungering child is crying for bread,
When Poverty walks the sorrowing land,
When Misery smites with murderous hand,
  O Sot, O Thou, of smouldering brain,
  Do sights, like these, give pleasure or pain?
  O Sot, O Thou, of maddening spell,
  Do sights, like these, betoken a hell?

Gone Before.

Gone before—
Closed the mystic door!
Soft the loved is sleeping,
Safe in holy keeping;
Cease the bitter weeping—
Only gone before!

Gone before—
Gained the unknown shore!
Hosts are gladly singing;
Harps are sweetly ringing;
Joy thro' heav'n is winging—
Only gone before!

Gone before —
Balm for hearts so sore!
O, forget your sorrow;
Smiles from dear hope borrow;
Loved you'll greet to-morrow —
Only gone before!

A POETIC PROPOSAL.

"O love, my love, my only love,
 Be now my own true wife,"
An ardent suitor whispered low,
 To one he prized as life;
"And then, as one, we'll gently glide
 Adown the stream of time;"—
To which the maiden calmly said:
 "Lord Byron wrote that rhyme."

"O love," he sighed, "my angel one,
 I worship none but you,
For in the round of all the earth,
 No other one's so true;
And should you cast my love aside,
 Despair would fill my breast;" —
To which the maiden gently said:
 "Those lines are Bulwer's best."

"O love," he moaned, "but lend a smile,
    And fame shall weave a spell,
To make the lips of wond'ring man,
    My worth and valor tell;
For, armed by thought and hope of you,
    I'll wage a war with wrong;"—
To which the maiden kindly said:
    "La me, that's Cowper's song."

"O love," he cried, "my peerless one,
    O sylph, with grace divine,
You do not dream the mighty flame
    Within this heart of mine;
For you I'd smite the shield of Death,
    Nor shrink to meet the fray;"—
To which the maiden softly said:
    "Tom Campbell tuned that lay."

"O love," he groaned, "I pray you speak,
 That I may know my fate,
And even now your magic voice
 Could open heaven's gate;
O yield your heart, seraphic one,
 I, bending, now implore;"—
To which the maiden sweetly said:
 "That strain was sung by Moore."

"You wicked witch," he fairly hissed,
 "I'd wed a shriveled shrew,
Before I'd be compelled to live
 With such an imp as you;
Besides, you're such a homely hag,
 Doré ne'er sketched a worse;"—
To which the maiden fondly said:
 "Why, Pet, that's Dante's verse."

HASTEN·

O hasten, my darling, while sunlight is streaming,
And tarry till moonlight, in glory, is beaming,
For welcome, unmeasured, is waiting to meet you,
And kisses, unnumbered, are longing to greet you.
Ah, truly, the skies have brightened above me,
Since hearing your vows and knowing you love me;
And even the birds, transported with pleasure,
Seem ever repeating: Come hither, my treasure.

I'll garland you gladly, with chaplet, so holy,
Of roses, so ruby, and lilies, so lowly;
I'll whisper you softly, a story inspiring,
Of loving forever, with ardor untiring.
As leaflet and bud awake in the shower,
My heart and my soul acknowledge your power;
As smiling of spring, each morning, grows brighter,
My spirit, my darling, in loving, grows lighter.

Enchanted, we'll wander in fairyland bowers,
Where angels are bending o'er ravishing flowers;
Enraptured, we'll hearken to music enthralling,
Where loudly the songster its sweetheart is calling.
O give me but love, unchangeably glowing,
And fountains of trust, unceasingly flowing,
And heaven, itself, with rapture, will quiver,
While safely, together, we're crossing life's river.

Power Divine.

The sheen of the morn,
    On the valley and mountain,
The gems of the field,
    And the gifts of the mine,
The glance of the rill,
    And the gleam of the fountain,
All tell, with their splendor,
    Of Power Divine.

The voice of the bird,
  In a rapture of gladness,
The sigh of the wind,
  Thro' the whispering pine,
The hush of the eve,
  With its shadow of sadness,
All tell, with their magic,
  Of Power Divine.

The tints of the wood,
  And their delicate blending,
The skirts of the cloud,
  And their mystical sign,
The Queen of the Night,
  And her armies attending,
All tell, with their beauty,
  Of Power Divine.

The blades of the storm,
    That the tempest is flashing,
The worlds that revolve
    In the hand of Design,
The wrath of the deep,
    When the billows are dashing,
All tell, with their grandeur,
    Of Power Divine.

O Light of all light,
    And the Source of all being,
The land and the sea
    And the heavens are Thine,
And over them all,
    And in wisdom decreeing,
Thou rulest forever,
    With Power Divine.

LIFE'S SERVICE.

In the morn of life,
When the sun is shining bright,
When the heart is beating light,
When the eyes are lit with glee,
When we sail the silv'ry sea,
We should look upon The One,
Who was slain on Calvary.

In the noon of life,
When the sun is throned on high,
When the days go swiftly by,
When the heart is bowed with care,
When we bend beneath despair,
We should call upon The One,
Who will all our burdens bear.

In the eve of life,
When the sun is sinking low,
When the arms aweary grow,
When for strength we vainly call,
When the friends around us fall,
We should lean upon The One,
Who has loving aid for all.

Just twenty years ago, my love,
　Just twenty years to-day,
As fairy blooms awoke, my love,
　At nudge of roguish May,
We gladly joined our hands, my love,
　And vowed to go as one,
Along the winding path, my love,
　That ends where life is done.

When compassed round by cares, my dear,
  Your faith has been the wand,
That cleft, for me, the way, my dear,
  Thro' seas of dark despond;
And when the clouds grew dark, my dear,
  And hid my sky from view,
I yet have found the light, my dear,
  When safe at home, with you.

When Doubt has thrown her spell, my love,
  You've smiled away my fears;
When Grief has wailed her dirge, my love,
  You've kissed away my tears;
And when my soul was bound, my love,
  With chains of gaunt Despair,
You've quickly loosed my bonds, my love,
  With words of hope and prayer.

It may perchance be true, dear one,
  As many sadly say,
That Time has touched your face, dear one,
  And tinged your hair with gray;
And yet, to me, it seems, dear one,
  That you are fairer now,
Than on that blushing morn, dear one,
  We made that holy vow.

But if your beauty fades, my love,
  At chilling touch of care,
And if the autumn frost, my love,
  Now steals upon your hair,
The lilies in your heart, my love,
  Yet bud and burst and blow,
As sweetly as they did, my love,
  A score of years ago.

Yet well, full well, we know, dear wife,
   Our Morn has wed the Noon,
And that we left them both, dear wife,
   Not far from land of June;
And Eve will shortly come, dear wife,
   With step as soft as light,
And gently lead us home, dear wife,
   To realms beyond the Night,

Behold, at eve, I found an asp,
Which then I took with kindly grasp,
And bore it hence with loving clasp,
But loose again with burning heart,
And brain that throbs with fevered start,
And eyes that pulse with fiery smart.

Behold, that asp, so stark and chill,
Once lonely lay on barren hill,
Where tempest voice was sharp and shrill,
While lurking doom about it prowled,
And frenzied wrath above it howled,
And glaring death anear it scowled.

Behold, with strange and youthful zest,
I fondly gave that serpent rest,
Upon my warm and trustful breast,
And then, by care, in princely store,
I wooed it back to life once more,
And kept it safe till night was o'er.

Behold, again, as morning sang,
And rosy light to heaven sprang,
That hooded asp, with deadly fang,
Gave silent stroke, with purpose fell,
To fill my veins with molten hell,
And chain my soul with dying spell.

Behold, that asp — Ingratitude —
That worst of all the devil's brood —
With cunning wile and malice shrewd,
Contrives to strike the venomed blow,
To lay the form of friendship low,
And blast the life where flowers grow.

I saw, to-day,
Some little ones play,
Who sung an old song as I passed,
And woke, for me,
By wand, of their glee,
A vision too sacred to last.

*   *   *

At eve, once more,
Again, as of yore,
My stocking I hung on the wall,
For well I knew
That Santa, so true,
Ere morning, with goodies, would call.

I heard, once more,
A threatening roar,
As Tempests, by Furies,
were led,
Yet gave no care,
For mother was there
To lovingly tuck me in bed.

With shouts, once more,
On glistening floor,
I galloped, astride of a broom,
And slid down stairs,
And jostled the chairs,
And frolicked in mother's
best room.

At school, once more,
I chiseled the door,
By aid of Bill Barlow, so
keen,
Then bounded out,
With echoing shout,
To sport on the beautiful green.

With sled, once more,
As often before,
Tho' sharp was the wintery air,
I climbed the hill,
With hearty good will,
For happiness waited me there.

And then, once more,
My trousers I tore,
When bending a sapling to ride,
But still no word,
Of sorrow, was heard,
Good clothing ne'er being my pride.

I sought, once more,
A hallowed shore,
And joyfully sprang in a stream,
Whose glad embrace,
And silvery face,
Bewitched like a beautiful dream.

But now, once more,
Those visions are o'er,
Whose magic illumined the sky;
And spring is dead,
And summer has fled,
And autumn-winds plaintively sigh.

O Dreams, so sweet,
The weary ye greet,
And woo them to Memory's bow'rs;
And robe thy views
In heavenly hues,
And border life's river with flow'rs.

MY O, my O, this sorry Hobo
Is simply a wreck, from top to the toe;
And wearily now, is pounding the road,
With speed of a mule, when yanking a load;
Yes, hitting the trail, with usual zeal,
To get to the East, to rustle a meal;
  And O, my O, this sorry Hobo
Is simply a wreck, from top to the toe.

And O, my O, this silly Hobo
Is fool number one, of fools that you know;
For surely he thought, when so he was told,
That here, at the front, were slathers of gold;
And so he cut loose, along with the rest,
And rode in the filth, away to the West;
And O, my O, this silly Hobo
Is fool number one, of fools that you know.

And O, my O, this luny Hobo
Then wanted to make a wonderful show;
So, waded in mud, and scolded and fussed,
And basted the mules, and shouted and cussed,
And rastled with bread, that surely was sad,
And tussled with meat, that truly was bad;
And O, my O, this luny Hobo
Then wanted to make a wonderful show.

And O, my O, this crazy Hobo
Soon went to the bad, as graders will go;
For when, by good luck, he chanced to be paid,
He reckoned that then, his fortune was made;
And so, to the dens, he hurried away,
And gambled by night, and guzzled by day;
And O, my O, this crazy Hobo
Soon went to the bad, as graders will go.

And O, my O, this bummy Hobo
Soon had for a bed, but beautiful snow;
For when, to the dives, his money had gone,
Like Wandering Jew, he had to move on;
And Poverty's foot then gave him a kick,
And many a tough repeated the trick;
And O, my O, this bummy Hobo
Soon had for a bed, but beautiful snow.

And O, my O, this busted Hobo
Now hustles to make this journey of woe;
For here, in the West, where grading is done,
There isn't a husk for Prodigal Son;
And sadly he says, nor should you forget,
That, under his belt, there's stomach to let;
And O, my O, this busted Hobo
Now hustles to make this journey of woe.

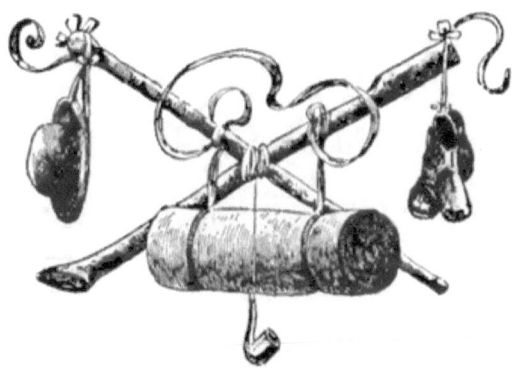

O THOU SUPREME.

MORNING SONG.

O Thou, Supreme,
 Thou Mighty One,
 With heavens for thy throne,
Be with us all, till life is done,
 Then claim us as Thine own.

EVENING SONG.

O Thou, Supreme,
 where seraphs throng,
 Enthroned above the night,
Give ear and hear our parting song,
 And lead us all to light.

THE CHILDREN'S HOUR.

IN MEMORY OF LONGFELLOW.

In the study, quaint and cozy,
  With its walls, by pictures hidden,
  With its shelves, by volumes laden,
  With its grate, by mantel sheltered,
  With its desk, by papers covered,
Sat the poet, lone and silent,
As the light with darkness dallied,
In the trysts where shadows gathered.
When, upon the winding stairway,
  With their cheeks, aglow with gladness,
  With their eyes, ablaze with gladness,
  With their voices, hushed to silence,
  With their footsteps, stilled to silence,

Came the children, tripping lightly,
Came the children, stealing softly,
  Lightly as the rosy morning,
  Softly as the dusky ev'ning,
Thro' the open doorway gliding,
  Gliding in as daylight loitered,
To the wide-armed chair, so restful,
Where, unmoving, deeply thinking,
Sat the poet as if sleeping.

Then, with glee, they pounced upon him,
And with shouts and peals of laughter,
  As upon his knees, they clambered,
  And about his neck they clustered,
Proudly called themselves his captors.

But the dear, the roguish darlings
Quickly found that fate was fickle,
For, instead of boasting captors,
They, ere long, were pleading pris'ners,
Held by giant arms so closely,
That they vainly strove for freedom.

Tired, at last, with useless striving,
  Striving vainly with their fetters,
They declared, in accents humble,
That, to gain, again, their freedom,
They would gladly give a ransom,

E'en a ransom from the treasure,
Given by their loving Father.

Then the proud and stalwart victor,
    Tho' full loth to loose the pris'ners,
    Yet more loth to lose the ransom,
Yielded to their princely offer;
But declared that captives, ever,
By the rules of lawless warfare,
    Such as they, the rogues, were waging,
Were required to pay the ransom,
Ere they gained again their freedom;
And that he would, therefore, never
Loose and free them from their fetters,
Till they paid to him the treasure
They had offered for their freedom.

Then, at once, they gave him freely,
From the wealth of priceless treasure,

Given by their loving Father,
Kisses, kisses, many kisses,
   Many, sweetest, purest kisses,
For of such was all the treasure,
Given by their loving Father.

Then the proud and stalwart victor,
   Well content to gain the ransom,
Loosed and freed them from the fetters,
That withheld, from them, their freedom.

But while yet the children lingered
Round the throne of their misfortune,
Conscience, clad in whitest raiment,
   White as robes the lofty mountains,
   White as robes the holy angels,
Came, as comes the lovely morning
   With its torch of love outholding,

Came, as comes the peaceful ev'ning
　　With its wand of peace outreaching,
And the victor thus admonished,
　　Gently, kindly, thus admonished:
Do not rob the darling children,
But return, to them, the ransom
You have taken from the treasure,
Given by their loving Father;
Victor, do not rob the children.

Then, much moved, he heard the whispers
Of the voice of white-robed Conscience,
And, rejoicing, gave the darlings
Kisses, kisses, many kisses,
　　Many, sweetest, purest kisses,
And returned, in full, the ransom
He had taken from the treasure,
Given by their loving Father.

Then away the children bounded,
  Like the stag, when horns are ringing,
  Like the hound, when prey is springing,
  Like the steed, when spurs are stinging,
Thus the darlings, laughing, shouting,
Bounded down the winding stairway,
Bearing with them all the treasure,
Given by their loving Father.

    *   *   *

All alone the poet waited,
In his study sat and waited,
  Waited as the day grew fainter,
  Waited as the shades grew deeper,
  Waited as the night grew darker,
Yet his eyes were filled with sunlight,
For his heart was filled with love-light.

Love's Moods

THE study of *Love*, tho'
    ever exciting,
Is deemed by us all,
    a study inviting;
For, in it, we read
    the story of kisses,
And, from it, we glean our holiest blisses.

The study of *Love*, has made
the world better,
And there is not one who is
not its debtor;
Ay, even the babe — that
cherub — rejoices,
Because, in its heart, there
whisper *Love's* voices.

I love and *I'm loved*, are lessons inspiring,
Which each of us cons, unwearied, untiring;
For learning *I love*, imparts a new pleasure,
And learning *I'm loved*, gives joy beyond measure.

The task we learn first, is *Love*, in the present,
And this is because *to love*, is so pleasant;
But shortly we find that loving is fleeting,
For often it flies, scarce heeding our greeting.

As learning *I love*, is often most vexing,
So learning *will love*, is often perplexing;
For Cupid, that elf, that wooer, so skilful,
Is often-times coy, and wayward and wilful.

And all of his aims, from mortals, are hidden,
Nor deigns he to do what mortals have bidden;
And ne'er do we learn that *Love* will steal round us,
Ere Cupid has caught and conquered and bound us.

The study of *Love*, is truly unending,
With numberless parts, distinct, and yet blending,
Presenting a view — one ever dissolving —
Of gladness and grief, together, revolving.

Yet lessons of *Love*, are ever enthralling,
No matter tho' tears, of sorrow, are falling;
But toil as we may, we master them never,
Till reaching that home where gladness reigns ever.

Wonderful river of Jordan,
  Calm is thy hallowed breast,
Whither the worn and the weary,
  Go unto infinite rest.

Wonderful river of Jordan,
  Hope of the many who mourn,
Never has wail of a sorrow,
  Waked thy mysterious bourn.

Wonderful river of Jordan,
  Bar to mortality's night,
Glory of Eden is shining,
  Flooding thy bosom with light.

Wonderful river of Jordan,
  Marge of the valley of time,
Lilies bend over thy border,
  Kist by the heavenly clime.

Wonderful river of Jordan,
  Stream where life's journey is o'er,
Silently bearing the lowly,
  Flow to the beautiful shore.

There is rest, true rest,
At the setting of the sun;
There is rest, true rest,
When the toiling all is done;
There is rest, true rest,
Safe within the pearly gates,
Where the mansion, over yonder,
For the weary, ever waits,

There is peace, sweet peace,
At the dawning of the day;
There is peace, sweet peace,
When the shadows fade away;
There is peace, sweet peace,
In the Temple of the Soul,
In that Holy of the Holies,
Where hosannas ever roll.

There is joy, glad joy,
When mortality is run;
There is joy, glad joy,
When eternity is won;
There is joy, glad joy,
When the great, angelic throng
Gives a greeting and a welcome
In a rhapsody of song.

O, Lord, we all, with joy, unite,
To ask, in faith, that wisdom's light,
May guide our feet in paths of right,
  And keep us close to Thee.

O, Lord, the lambs that chance to stray,
Of prowling wolves are soon the prey;
So guard us all by night and day,
  And keep us close to Thee.

O, Lord, thou One whose love we sing,
And whose dear Gift gave gladness wing,
Within our lives make beauty spring,
   And keep us close to Thee.

O, Lord, when all our work is done,
And wearied hands sweet rest have won,
Take Thou us all, rejecting none,
   And keep us close to Thee.

Holding aloft the banner of right,
Keeping its folds forever in sight,
Falter we not, tho' dangers are near,
Murmur we not, tho' heavens are drear.

Gathering faith from promise of God,
Having no fear of chastening rod,
Bravely we march to shadows of night,
Gladly we march to dawning of light.

Claiming the help of Infinite One,
Firmly resolved no duty to shun,
Gladness we bring to many who mourn,
Courage we bring to weary and worn.

Firm in the faith, we journey along,
Waking the notes of hallowed song;
Singing of hope, when trials begin,
Singing of joy, when battles we win.

Tho' glad hearts are beating,
  And the joy-notes ring,
Old Time now is fleeting,
  With a well-poised wing;
And soon we will sever,
  With a warm "good night,"
And thoughts that will ever,
  Make the eyes grow bright;
And, friends, tho' as strangers,
  On the paths you tread,

I hope that no dangers
  May be crouched o'erhead;
And when, on the morrow,
  Holy night - fall nears,
I trust that no sorrow
  Will arouse your fears;
And pray that your rivers,
  When your course you've run,
May tell, by their quivers,
  Of a fair - set sun.

You may talk about the many
   In the race to gain the skies,
And may even name the sinners,
   You declare to win the prize,
But if zeal, in matters holy,
   Can, for sin, at all, atone,
Bear in mind that bronco-riders
   Won't be last to reach the throne.

As you know, I left the college,
    In the spring of 'eighty-one,
With the wish to preach the Gospel,
    Out beneath the setting sun;
So, I wandered to the westward,
    Where the tide of empire rolls,
Seeking place to serve the Master,
    At the work of saving souls.

Well, by hap, the wheel of fortune,
    Steered me out upon the plain,
Where, it seemed, the mighty Reaper,
    Scarce would think to look for grain;
For the crop was thin and scanty,
    Yet would grow so very tall,
That, when Satan raised a tempest,
    It was sure to lodge or fall.

But, altho' the earth seemed arid,
    And, in spots, was nearly bare,
And, altho' the harvest Sower,
    Scattered wheat but here and there,
Still, the stalks, if few in number,
    Often gave a goodly yield,
Even tho' the storms of error,
    Swept, at times, across the field.

For the seed would never wither,
  Mattered not how poor the land,
As the lowly germs were planted,
  By a mother's magic hand;
And would therefore spring to beauty,
  In despite of drouths and rust,
And return a golden fruitage,
  For the garner of the Just.

And, of course, upon that prairie,
  On that wide and waveless sea,
Where the skies, in moving splendor,
  Span such vast eternity,
Man would grow in will and power,
  Man would gain in soul and brawn,
And the one, at heart, a coward,
  Found it best to gallop on.

Well, just why, I'll never tell you,
　　But I liked those buccaneers,
Who so madly rode that ocean,
　　In the wake of Texan steers;
So, I sharply veered my rudder,
　　Fully bent to change my tack,
And was soon as wild a cowboy,
　　As bestrode a bronco's back.

But, one day, the others reckoned—
　　Just as tho' they didn't care—
That my gift was surely preaching,
　　Seeing how I couldn't swear;
And, one eve, as fairy visions,
　　From the past, came trooping in,
They declared it was my duty,
　　There, with them, to wrestle sin.

Quickly, then, the touch of Conscience,
　　Roused me from my slothful sleep,
While a spirit voice repeated
　　Holy vows I'd failed to keep;
When, at once, with strange emotion,
　　Moved, somehow, by wizard spell,
I arose and told the story,
　　Each had heard his mother tell.

Cared I not, that hour, for glory,
　　Spoke I not of carping creed,
Nor, to words of worldly wisdom,
　　Gave I then a moment's heed;
But I simply led my hearers,
　　'Mid the mob, beneath the tree,
Where the One, of love and mercy,
　　Died, for them, on Calvary.

Ere my simple tale was finished,
  Many eyes were filled with tears,
And upon no lip was resting,
  E'en the trace of cynic sneers;
Later still, when praise was offered,
  Many sung that song of yore:
Come, ye sinners, poor and needy,
  Weak and wounded, sick and sore.

Now, it chanced that one, queer fellow,
   Left the crowd as I begun,
Stating that he choosed to vanish,
   Till that pious chap was done;
Whereupon the rest concluded,
   It was best to teach him, then,
That, when others talked religion,
   He should say, at least, "Amen."

So, when service all had ended,
   Plunged they him, by law of might,
In a pool of muddy water,
   Claiming thus they served him right;
And as forth he blindly scrambled,
   Of all sights about the worst,
Gave they him a second sousing,
   So he'd know he'd been immersed.

Therefore, when you count the many
  In the race to gain the skies,
And are pointing out the sinners,
  You declare to win the prize,
Bear in mind, if zeal is worthy,
  And, for sin, may e'er atone,
Then the rider of the bronco,
  Won't be last to reach the throne.

When wave is silvern, and the clouds are few,
And keel is oaken, and the spars are new,
If Love go with us o'er the boundless blue,
     We'll gain Eternity.

When sky is sullen, and the winds are cold,
And flock is straying, and the wolves are bold,
If lambs we gather, for the Lord's great fold,
     We'll gain Eternity.

When sea is surging, and the sails are torn,
And hulk is straining, and the ropes are worn,
If cares, of others, in our hearts, are borne,
    We'll gain Eternity.

When strength is fallen, and the years are run,
And work is ended, and the strifes are done,
If sins we've battled, and the fights we've won,
    We'll gain Eternity.

THE SOD HOUSE COMING.

The pioneer, on Western plain,
    Requires more nerve and daring,
Than they who step to martial strain,
    Or Valor's plumes are wearing;
For he may claim but walls of sod,
    Tho' storms be wildly raving,
And Want full often plies the rod,
    As Fate he's sternly braving;

And you, of love, when hours you while,
  As cars go westward humming,
Fling out a kiss, and wing a smile,
  When you see the sod house coming.

The pioneer, on boundless plain,
  Has stirred the wilds to duty,
For deserts now, bear golden grain,
  And witch the eye with beauty;
And there, within the humble homes,
  Diviner notes are ringing,
Than wake the aisles of stately domes,
  When choirs are proudly singing;
And you, of pride, when hours you while,
  As cars go westward humming,
Bend low your heads, nor dare revile,
  When you see the sod house coming.

The pioneer, on treeless plain,
  Should live in song and story,
And far across the rolling main,
  Should speed his name of glory;
For never yet to peaceful strife,
  Went forth more valiant foeman,
Nor ever yet, on field of life,
  Has strived more sturdy yeoman;
And you, of fame, when hours you while,
  As cars go westward humming,
Slow down your train, and lift your tile,
  When you see the sod house coming.

Whene'er we meet at restful eve,
As hands unseen the shadows weave,
We speed the wings of fading light,
Then smiling say: Good night, good night:
Ah me, those words are like the mist,
That burning lips to skies have kist,
To breathe again, in wizard rain,
And woo from earth her sweetest strain.

And when, afar, we're called to roam,
To soon return to friends and home,
Before we go, we barely sigh,
Tho' loth to say: Good-by, good-by;
Ah me, those words, like flecks of gray,
That slowly sail their silv'ry way,
But robe the vales, with richer glow,
Where rippling rills of kindness flow.

And when we're doomed by fate to part
From those we shrine in love's dear heart,
We seem to hear the mournful bell,
As sad we say: Farewell, farewell;
Ah me, those words are like the clouds,
That hang, on high, like ghostly shrouds,
While wailing winds of sorrow blow,
And Joy, herself, lies wrapped in snow.

But when we say: Good night, good night,
Those fleecy words, in bridal white,
Or softly call: Good-by, good-by,
Those dusky words, in azure sky,
Or sadly breathe: Farewell, farewell,
Those sable words, with wintry spell,
We feel that yet our winding ways
Will cross, somewhere, in coming days.

NOTES.

Note 1, Page 13.—THE COWBOY.

Reckless and tireless, untamable as a prairie chicken, brave as proudest knight in storied tourney, the Cowboy is the dauntless hero of a new chivalry, even more strange and romantic than that of the middle ages.

In speaking *to* a comrade, he calls him *waddy;* when talking *of* one, he refers to him as *puncher*.

Note 2, Page 24.—BEN.

This poem, while relating an experience of the writer, is intended to show that, even in the most calloused heart, there is goodness which the talismanic name of *Mother*, at times will awaken.

The terms used are: *Budge*—whiskey; *navy*—revolver; *steamed above his gauge*—drank to excess; *plug the imp*—shoot him.

Note 3, Page 42.—MAVERICK JOE.

Col. Maverick, of Texas, who owned a very large number of cattle, allowed them to stray over the plains unclaimed—because of which, the cattlemen finally came to calling every unbranded animal a *Maverick*. Naturally, when Texan stock were driven North, the term mentioned went with them, until now it is actually engrafted on the Statutes of some of the Western States, like meaning being given it as in the place of its origin.

As the cow and calf never fail to recognize each other, the latter, of course, is given the same brand as that of its mother. Hence, the only way of preventing the true ownership of the calf from being known, is to separate it from the cow, to do which, the latter is not infrequently killed by the *rustlers* or *Maverick thieves.*

In the poem, Maverick Joe marked a lone calf with his cross (+). On the next day, at the round-up, the mother, branded with a square (⊐), was driven in, when followed the recognition and consequences pictured out in the lines.

The terms used in the poem are: *Bronco-buster* — one who breaks broncos; *puncher* — a cattle-driver; *rangher* — a horse-herder; *whisper* — to talk loudly, one who does so, being called a *whisperer; rustle* — to steal; *tenderfoot* — one unused to the west; *budge* — whiskey; *rastled* — wrestled; *round-up* — the driving in together of all the cattle from a large territory, participated in by all owners, each of whom then brands the stock to which he is entitled, the calf being given a like brand, as that borne by the mother.

Note 4, Page 51.—THEN.

A young lady, sad because of a broken engagement, asked that a poem be written, to be entitled, *Then and Now.*

As the chief charm of poetry is due to the fact that, within it, there is ever a hiatus for the mind of the reader to fill, the title of *Then* was found to be amply sufficient for the entire thought desired, the *Now* being but slightly concealed between the lines.

Note 5, Page 54.—THE PRAIRIE-DOG.

The occasion of these lines was the following incident: Riding with a friend, in Wyoming, the writer remarked that a poem might be found in any subject, if the seeker had only the necessary skill. To this, the other replied by saying that there was no poetry in a prairie-dog, at the same time pointing to one, a little distant, which was then sitting proudly upright, barking and jerking its tail vigorously.

In regard to the prairie-dog, it is to be remarked: (1) That it invariably moves its tail every time it barks, the tail apparently being the lever by which its jaws are moved; (2) that it is seemingly one of the proudest and happiest of all those accustomed to village or city life; (3) that the snake and owl invariably inhabit its burrow, probably for the purpose of dining upon its young; and (4) that it never makes its home by a pond or stream, preferring to dig to water rather than run the risk of a damp bed or being flooded out.

Note 6, Page 68.—My Dream of Love.

An old man, with whom the writer is acquainted, invariably calls a certain young lady, "My Dream of Love," alone because of the resemblance she bears to the wife of his young manhood, who, tho' gone before, yet remains his dream of love. Hence this poem.

Note 7, Page 70.—The Blizzard.

The blizzard of January 12, 1888 — the worst that ever swept across the western plains — was made historic by the three Nebraska school-ma'ams, the deeds of whom are incidentally referred to in this poem. The story, however, of the saving of the father by the boy's ringing of the bell — told the writer by Mr. Jay Burrows, of Lincoln, Neb., and here published for the first time — is an incident certainly no less noteworthy than the others alluded to, and furnishes a theme which it would require the genius of a Scott to fittingly portray.

It may be that exception will be taken to the line, "*She held four kings at the game of prayer.*" If so, the reader is asked to remember that, at poker, one holding such a hand, would — upon the ratio of chances — scarcely lose once in a thousand times. Hence, the line, as written, is a forcible, tho' rough statement of the fact that the wife's prayer was so earnest and potent, that it could not well fail to accomplish its purpose. Besides, it should be borne in mind that the tale is told in the west, and therefore it can not be said to be improper to couch it in the vigorous words not infrequently used in many parts of that breezy section of country.

Again, it may be that exception will also be taken to the fact that the speaker, tho' evidently an educated person, is made to use slang. To such criticism, the answer is given that even the newest portions of the west are peopled with men, who, tho' from the schools and colleges of the east, yet habitually use slang — not because they do not know how to speak elegantly, but simply because, by slang, they may abridge their words and add emphasis without abridging their meaning or running the risk of not being understood. Indeed, the one who makes even the wildest of these western people appear as unlettered boors, not only fails to understand the people of whom he writes, but actually does injustice to that great country for which he presumes to speak.

Note 8, Page 95.—INYAN KARA.

In the volcanic age, during which the great west was first a sea of water and then a sea of fire, a new mountain was upheaved thro' the very center of an older one, leaving but the rim of the latter intact, which still grimly encircles its rocky usurper. This curious formation stands in the northeast corner of Wyoming, on the margin of a vast plain, and is known by the Indian name of *Inyan Kara,* meaning a mountain within a mountain. Some miles away, across the flats, the Sundance mountain lifts its bald brow, where of yore the youthful warrior demonstrated his courage as well as his indifference to pain, by the bloody test of the far-famed, yet horrid, Sun Dance.

Arla is the Crow name for *arm*, Eeka meaning *pretty*. The latter term, however, is usually written *Ichie*. Still, as this method only misleads the reader, in regard to the proper pronunciation, and as there is really no standard for the writing of Indian names, it has been thought best to print it just as it should be pronounced.

Note 9, Page 105. - HIGH MASS OF THE MUSES.

For fifty years, Prof. Mendal had presided over that greatest of church organs---the one at Berne, Switzerland. For the purpose of attracting visitors, the authorities threw open the doors of the great Cathedral, during the tourist season, furnishing free entertainment to all who cared to attend.

One lovely evening, with the idling crowd, the writer was swept into the magnificent minster, just as the shadows of the Alps were falling across the valleys of that wonderland. In the great room and almost hidden within the groined vaulting, a half dozen feeble tapers lent their flickering rays, not for the purpose of giving light, but only to add more of weirdness to the scene and make the darkness even more sensibly apparent. Presently the familiar melody, "*Must I Depart From My Mountains,*" began to steal thro' the silent chamber, as if from the lips of some divine Diva, the soprano being in turn succeeded by alto, bass and tenor voices, each, in succession, taking up and repeating the same simple strain. Then, just as the last note seemed dying away, the song again came pulsing thro' the shadowy darkness, the notes of all the singers being blent and melted into a chorus of moving power and wondrous beauty, to which a myriad of wind and stringed instruments lent their softest strains, all trilling forth enchanting variations of that same Tyrolean lay. Shortly, a far-away peal of thunder half-startled the entranced throng, the distant rumble being quickly followed by louder and more threatening warnings of the nearing tempest. Soon the air began to sigh and, ere long, to whistle thro' the stately corridors of that majestic temple of the muses, the storm being hurried along by the winds rushing from the organ's lungs. But these sounds were soon lost in the rhythmic roar of a classical tornado, which then came charging on, fairly shaking the building in its mad wrath, despite of which ever crept out the beautiful notes of that Alpine song. Then, again, the storm began to abate, even as woods of feathered songsters come forth, and, in snatches of that same simple melody, warbled praise to the hidden Apollo, who, high-perched in the organ-loft, had lifted a cloud from many a heart of many a listening dreamer. Then, once more, a choir, seemingly of sweet voiced singers, took up that mountain melody, and, wander-

ing farther and farther away, sung it over and over again,
while the enraptured throng bent forward to catch the last
lingering cadence of the expiring rhapsody. O, it was
glorious! Ay, that song was even more enchanting than
ever a siren wafted winningly across the wave to woo a
Ulysses upon the mythical breakers of the Caprean rocks.

When the writer spoke to that master, in eulogy of the
performance, the latter modestly replied: "*Ah, the instru-
ment is a very fine one.*"

High mass is a religious service, entirely of music.

Note 10, Page 120.—THE LOON CRY.

The loon — that swiftest swimmer of all the feathered
tribe — cries in a minor key, and seems to say, "*Only a fool
I see!*"

Note 11, Page 131.—A THIRTY YEARS' DREAM.

The writer, returning to his native home after an ab-
sence of many years, found that the little country school-
house, attended by him in youth, had been torn away, and
a railroad constructed across the very spot where it had
stood. Hence, this poem, addressed to Alf. Mattix, a former
school-mate

Note 12, Page 152.—THE CURLEW SONG.

The Curlew Song, tho' moving but a single step of the
gamut, and that by half tones, is not unmusical, and,

beside, can be easily imagined as saying the words attributed to it in the poem.

And, here, by the way, it might not be amiss to state that this poem was written far out on the western plain, the prompter being a curlew, which, untried and unvexed by business cares, and uncaged and unbruised by a torturing stage-coach, sailed gracefully on before, on arching wing, singing its simple lay—one seemingly begotten of a happiness far exceeding that possessed by the ordinary run of human-kind.

Note 13, Page 163.—BAIT.

The following incident was the occasion of this poem: At a recent session of the Nebraska Legislature, the number of employes on the rolls was strikingly large, almost every committee having its paid clerk, such appointment being made for the sole purpose, generally speaking, of giving some friend of the chairman a sinecure position at the expense of the State. Hon. John C. Watson —one of the leaders of the minority party and who, two years before, had been the presiding officer of the same House—was appointed chairman of the Fish Committee, this position being given him as a mere joke, there being nothing whatever for this committee to do. Shortly after this, Mr. Watson arose and solemnly asked that the presiding officer allow him a clerk. Greatly astonished at such a request, the Speaker sharply demanded to know what possible use the chairman of the Fish Committee had for a Clerk, to which query, instantly came back the apt and satirical answer: "*To cut bait.*"

Note 14, Page 172.—HAVE I THY LOVE.

These lines are a translation of the German song, "*Hab' Ich nur Deine Liebe*," written by Zell and Genée, for the operetta, *Boccaccio.* This quaint poem has heretofore generally been considered as untranslatable.

Note 15, Page 199.—LIFE'S AFTERNOON.

This poem was written for, and read on the occasion of the twentieth anniversary of the wedding of Rev. Eli Fisher and wife, then residing at Beatrice, Nebraska.

Note 16, Page 211.—HOBO'S LAMENT.

The origin of *Hobo*, the term now so generally applied to the railroad grader, is unknown, but is generally supposed to have come from the salutation of "Ho, boy!" which was shouted by one workman to another, and finally shortened into the name now in common use. The Hobos are enlisted, so to speak, by labor agents, in the larger of the western cities and shipped, in car-loads, to the points where wanted. Naturally, as may well be imagined, the Hobo-car, long ere it reaches its destination, is redolent with odors not of those which are said to be clinging to the garments of the fair daughters of Farina. The Hobo is, or soon becomes, a queer type of humanity. Earning good wages, he toils contentedly on, despite rain and mud, till the monthly payday comes. Then he takes a lay-off for the purpose of spending his wealth, at which he is a phenomenal success. Indeed, as illustrative of this assertion, mention is here made of the fact that, upon one occasion, where a large number of such laborers were given their pay-checks, *ninety per cent.* of their entire earnings was held and owned by the adjacent saloons, dens of infamy and gambling hells, before the next sunrise. After a reasonable time spent in such debauchery, they are willing again to return to work, seemingly only hoping for another pay-day to arrive, to bring with it a repetition of its insane orgies and fancied lelights.

The meaning of the terms used in this poem, are: *Pounding the road*—walking the road; *rustle a meal*—hunting something to eat; *hitting the trail*—footing homeward; *slathers of gold*—abundance of money; *cut loose along with the rest*—went with them; *basted the mules*—pounded them; *rastled with bread*—wrestled with, or worried it down; *hustles*—walks earnestly.

Note 17, Page 237. THE COWBOY PREACHER.

The story of the two-fold ducking of the cowboy who

refused to remain to hear the sermon, relates an actual incident which took place in Wyoming.

Note 18, Page 248.—THE SOD HOUSE COMING.

Mr. C. E. Perkins, President of the Chicago, Burling-
ton & Quincy Railroad Company, recently made a tour of
his lines of road, accompanied by his wife and a party of
friends.

Mrs. Perkins, on this occasion, kindly took with her a
large assortment of toys and picture books, with which to
gladden the little ones, whom she should chance to see on
her journey. Observing these presents, as they were placed
aboard the train, Mr. Perkins dryly remarked that the
engineer should go slow, whenever the latter saw a sod
house coming, reference being to the fact that the gifts
were intended only for the children of the prairies, and
hence opportunity should be given for their distribution.

On such pleasure jaunts, Mrs. Perkins takes with her
a log-book, for which a member of the party is asked to
contribute something pertaining to the trip; the article, in
this instance, was requested of the writer, this poem
being the response.

SPECIAL NOTE.

Many of the illustrations in this work, are by James Cady, of Beatrice, Neb., the remainder being the handiwork of Hugo Schulz, of Chicago, Ill.